Dempsey and Makepeace
LOVE YOU TO DEATH

D0754006

Also available from Futura

JACK SAVAGE

Dempsey and Makepeace
LOVE YOU TO DEATH

Based on an original screenplay
by Roger Marshall

Futura

A Futura Book

Series created by Golden Eagle Films
Novelization copyright © Jack Savage/
Macdonald & Co (Publishers) Ltd 1986

First published in Great Britain in 1986 by
Futura Publications, A Division of
Macdonald & Co (Publishers) Ltd
London & Sydney

All characters in this publication are fictitious
and any resemblance to real persons, living or dead,
is purely coincidental.

All rights reserved.
No part of this publication may be reproduced,
stored in a retrieval system, or transmitted, in any
form or by any means without the prior
permission in writing of the publisher, nor be
otherwise circulated in any form of binding or
cover other than that in which it is published and
without a similar condition including this
condition being imposed on the subsequent
purchaser.

ISBN 0 7088 3157 5

Typeset by Leaper & Gard Ltd, Bristol, England
Printed and bound in Great Britain by
Cox & Wyman, Reading

Futura Publications
A Division of
Macdonald & Co (Publishers) Ltd
Greater London House
Hampstead Road
London NW1 7QX
A BPCC plc Company

MAY 23 1991

Chapter
ONE

Theodore Barret's alarm clock went off at twenty minutes past seven precisely. He knew that it was precise because he set it by the Greenwich time signal every Sunday. He let it ring three times and then silenced it with a smooth movement of his arm followed by a swift type with his index finger on the upstanding red button. Occasionally he let it ring four times and occasionally twice but three times was the average.

Theodore Barret liked averages. He was in life insurance and it was important for him to have lots of averages at his fingertips. He knew, for instance, that short bald men died on average one year younger than those of average height with an average head of hair. If they sweated more than average then you could take another six months off that. His company, the London Mutual Assurance, didn't have separate policies for short bald men who sweated a lot, of course. It might make short bald men who sweated a lot rather angry and besides many of their most valued customers, not to mention many of their own employees, were short bald men who sweated a lot. But what it did mean was that average people of average height, with an average head of hair, who sweated averagely, people like Theodore Barret himself in fact, were being made to pay for all those short bald and sweaty premature stiffs.

Theodore Barret smiled for a moment at the idea of calling the recently deceased holder of a life insurance policy a stiff. But, on second thoughts, perhaps this wasn't quite so amusing. His profession had changed a great deal since he first entered it eighteen years ago. Everyone was trying to be American. Young men almost half his age, whom he hardly knew, used to slap him on the back in th corridor and pretend that they were the greatest of friends. Some even called him Theo, an abbreviation that he detested. So perhaps the day wasn't too far away when clients would be approached with a cheerful 'But have you thought of what will happen to your family if you should unfortunately become a stiff?' Still Theodore hoped that he wouldn't be alive to see that day.

He swung his legs out of bed and slid his feet into his slippers. He crossed the landing, entered the bathroom and turned on the light in order to examine the night's aging in the mirror. He decided that he looked much the same as he did every morning and even though he was thirty-eight now he couldn't remember ever having looked any different. Aging was a gradual process and he was glad that it was. He imagined what it would be like if one didn't age, say between birthdays, but then on every birthday one aged a whole year. It would be frightening. He stopped imagining it and brushed his teeth instead. Teeth brushed, he lifted up his upper lip and examined his teeth in the mirror. Facially Theodore

Barret was what is normally referred to as plain, plain meaning slightly ugly, but his slight ugliness was offset by the most magnificent set of teeth. His dentist said that they were the finest teeth that he had ever seen. Theodore suspected that he said that to everyone. But none the less examining them in the mirror this morning he was forced to admit that they really were pretty fine. They were beautifully regular and brilliantly white and they seemed to smile all by themselves.

Bathroom duties performed, Theodore dressed. He wore the clothes that he always wore on Monday, they looked exactly the same as the clothes that he wore every other day of the working week but *he* knew that they were his Monday clothes and that was all that mattered. They consisted of a dark grey suit, a stripy blue shirt and a red tie with white polka dots on. Not only did they look like the clothes that he wore every other day of the working week, they looked like the clothes everyone else wore every other day of the working week. Everyone in life insurance at least. The image was completed by a well-polished pair of leather brogues.

June, Theodore's wife, slept on as he went through his dressing ritual. Ready to face the day, Theodore lent over and woke her with a kiss. It was always one kiss and always on the left cheek, and no matter how light it was it always seemed to wake her. It woke her today. She rolled over and smiled at her husband warmly. There was no need for words. For both of them their marriage was like a dream come true, a fairy tale. Theodore made his way downstairs as June climbed out of bed and began to dress.

George heard Theodore tiptoeing down the stairs and eagerly anticipated his arrival by vigorous waggings of his tail. Theodore bent down and wrestled with

7

him briefly in the hall. Then taking the dog's lead off the coat-hook, he attached it to George's collar and opened the front door.

It was a magnificent morning. Spring was turning into summer, the air was fresh and the light was clear. The low sun flashed between the trees as the two of them walked along. Even the constant hum of London's traffic seemed to be slightly subdued this morning, perhaps it was in awe of this sudden display of nature's wonders thought Theodore to himself. Secretly he was a bit of a romantic, though only his family were allowed to see this side of him.

Theodore breathed in the air like a general and George pulled on the lead like his horse, even though he was no more than a basset hound. They were off to the park as usual and it was difficult to say who enjoyed the daily pilgrimage most. For both of them it was really their only chance in the day to get away from it all. Theodore could be secretly romantic and George could hunt rabbits. There were no rabbits in the park of course; it was only a small park set in the middle of the built-up suburb in which Theodore lived. Most of it was formally arranged, but there were sections that were less visited where nature had been allowed to take its course. It was to one of these sections of the park that Theodore and George were making. They passed beneath the window of Dempsey's apartment.

Inside Dempsey was still asleep, oblivious of the warm sunlight that streamed through his bedroom window. Normally he'd have been up at this hour as well, but he'd had a dreadful night the night before.

He'd been to a friend's party and he'd met a woman there who he'd taken a shine to. She didn't have a chip on her shoulder about Americans, not like many of the English women that he could mention, and there seemed to be a fair amount of mutually reciprocated physical attraction between them. Well Dempsey wanted to sleep with her anyway. He had contemplated giving her the line about being an international oil executive, but looking at her again she seemed to be too nice to lie to. So he had told her the truth, that he was a cop. This was a big mistake. She had dropped him like he was a contagious disease and what's more she told everyone else that he was catching. Dempsey was made to feel like a Nazi at a barmitzvah. He decided that she definitely wasn't too nice to lie to. He also decided that he wouldn't let himself be frozen out by these stupid people with their absurd prejudices against policemen, and so he stuck out the party until the bitter end, that is until the bitter ran out.

He left with dignity, but he found his way home with some difficulty. When he got home and lay down he had the spins for about an hour before he could get to sleep and then he woke up again at three in the morning desperately in need of a glass of water. He slept soundly now, though, through one of the few bright moments of the much maligned British weather.

Theodore strolled on, his stride so casual it was almost a swagger. His reverie and rhythm were interrupted, however, by the sudden appearance of Catherine Warren on the pavement in front of him. She had stepped out from behind the uplifted bonnet of a car that she seemed to be mending. Recovering his bearings, Theodore smiled at her and would have tipped his hat if he'd been wearing one. She smiled back, looking completely unflustered by their near collision. What a wonderful morning thought Theodore to himself, it could even turn the anti-social Londoner into something approaching a gregarious human being. He walked on. Catherine Warren carefully shut the bonnet of the car that she had been working on and watched Theodore and George's progress down the street. His apparent happiness annoyed her. She was unhappy; thirty, petite, brown-haired and unhappy. On top of this she was sick, sick in heart and mind. She picked up the briefcase and the carrier bag that she had left beside the car and set off towards the park, following Theodore and George. She looked like any other thirty year old, brown-haired, petite, unhappy woman. For her it was a beautiful day also, but it was beautiful for very different reasons.

George didn't really notice how beautiful the day was. He didn't really care. Theodore took him for a walk come rain or shine. Though on days like today he did tend to linger a little longer.

The park, when they arrived, looked resplendent. The combination of light, dew and air made everything seem somehow more alive. The feeling communicated itself to Theodore, he felt younger than he'd done for years. He drank in the atmosphere until he was full to the brim. He should have brought June, Kate and little Annie along to witness this magnificent morning. He decided that he would pick some flowers and try to take some of the morning back to them. He made his way towards the most unkempt corner of the park, where the undergrowth was most tangled and occasionally wild flowers were to be found. As he did so, he thought he saw a small black-clad figure flit between the trees. Yes, there it

10

was again. He stood motionless for a moment trying to catch another glimpse. He was reminded of his youth in the country when he used to go badger spotting in the very early morning with his father. But there were no badgers here and the figure didn't reappear either. Perhaps it was a ghost. Perhaps it was the black-clad figure of Death itself.

Theodore smiled at the far-fetched nature of his imagination for the second time that day. The fresh air seemed to have made him almost drunk. He wondered what they would do in the office if they heard him talking of ghosts and 'the black-clad figure of Death itself'. They would probably laugh he thought. Though they might like to give the black-clad figure a job interview; death would be quite a useful employee for a life insurance company, even if only to put the competition out of business. He toyed with the thought for a moment longer and then remembered that he'd decided to pick some flowers. He set about doing so and he filed the figure in black under 'kids' and 'harmless fun'.

But the figure in black was neither a kid nor bent upon harmless fun. The figure in black was Catherine Warren. She had arrived at the park only a few seconds after Theodore and George and had sneaked past them in order to find the most secluded and secure spot. There she had changed out of her ordinary clothes, a light cotton skirt and a T-shirt, into what could only be described as a cat-burglar's outfit. She left her other clothes where she had changed and emerged wearing a black track suit, a black balaclava and black gloves. She was still carrying the briefcase. She looked a strange figure, dressed totally in black on such a bright and warm morning. But fortunately, or perhaps unfortunately, no one

11

saw her apart from Theodore. Suspecting that he had seen her, Catherine observed Theodore through the trees for quite some time before moving off. When he bent down and began to search for something in the grass her interest was aroused but she soon realized that he was doing nothing more interesting than picking flowers. She made her way towards the end of the park. Even the way that she moved seemed designed to draw attention to herself. She ran between the trees like a villain in a Laurel and Hardy film, pausing behind each one to check whether the coast was clear.

But Catherine Warren was anything but a comic character. In fact Theodore Barret had been far nearer the mark when he had thought of her as Death. She wasn't Death of course, or at least she wasn't Death in the 'grim reaper' sense. She was more like one of his sales staff, for in her slim black briefcase she was carrying a precision, high-calibre 7.62mm rifle and in her mad mind she harboured thoughts of murder. It was a potent combination.

Theodore continued gathering flowers; for him murders only happened in books, books and the worst kind of television programmes. He very seldom went to the movies nowadays. George began to bark at something. He thought he'd found a rabbit, but it turned out to be a tramp.

Catherine reached the end of the park. A wire fence about eight foot high separated it from the yard of an anonymous looking nineteen-sixties warehouse. She climbed the fence quickly and nimbly and dropped down on the other side. She crouched low for a moment, looking and listening to find out whether anyone had seen or heard her. Nothing stirred. She ran across the yard to the base of the warehouse. She checked the fire-escape. It wasn't locked. The factory had obviously had a recent visit from the local fire officer and they hadn't bothered to lock it up properly again. She climbed it. She felt that her luck was in, or was it just luck, perhaps some divine hand had opened the fire-escape door for her so she could fulfil her mission? She reached the top of the stairs and pushed against the door that led to the roof. It opened easily.

The roof was flat and covered with asphalt and a thin sprinkling of gravel. Catherine walked to the edge and looked out over the park. She could just make out, between the trees, Theodore Barret still gathering flowers. She looked down at the ground, it was a long way to fall. A sudden chill crept over her as if the devil had just walked across her grave, but it soon passed. She walked to the opposite side of the roof. On that side the warehouse faced a road. A bus approached along it and stopped at the bus stop just opposite where she was standing. No one got on or off and the bus pulled away up the street and disappeared round the corner. Catherine stood there and smiled, but the smile gave away nothing. Anyone could have seen her standing up there, but no one did. She sat down, leaning against the short wall of the roof, and waited.

By this time Theodore had gathered a nice, large bunch of flowers. He stood up and admired them, twisting them in his hand. They were mostly dandelions and cow-parsley, though he had managed to find some of those small blue flowers with yellow eyes whose name he couldn't quite remember and a couple of purple ones whose name he'd never known. He called for George as it was time for them to be getting back. George burst out of the bushes and hurtled towards his master, he was very wet. Putting the lead on him again Theodore worried if June might not be cross with him for bringing back the dog in such a sodden state, but he wasn't too muddy so Theodore reckoned that it would probably be alright.

They made their way home, Theodore proudly holding out his flowers in front of him and George looking forward to his breakfast. They passed beneath Dempsey's bedroom window again.

Inside Dempsey was still asleep. He'd woken up about ten minutes ago but his alarm clock had read only twenty-minutes-past seven and so he had decided to go back to sleep again. Now he was in that marvellous period of sleep when days can be dreamt of in seconds and waking is so close that nightmares can be escaped from at will.

But at present Dempsey had no desire to escape from his dreams, because at present he was dreaming of Makepeace. She'd just asked him whether he thought that he was man enough to love her in a tone of voice that he'd never heard her use in real life and doubted whether he ever would. She was definitely trying to seduce him. He walked towards her slowly, his pulse quickening. Their lips met and as they did so she dug her long painted fingernails into the rippling muscles of his back. She was just about to ... but the only trouble with that period of sleep when nightmares can be escaped from at will is that waking is really too close. The conscious mind that allows you to wake up from nightmares, because they are too implausible, will also wake you up on occasion in pleasantly implausible situations. The two of them making love was one such situation.

Dempsey opened his eyes slowly. He was annoyed. Whenever he dreamt about Makepeace this happened. He wasn't even positive that he dreamt about Makepeace because he fancied her. In many respects she embodied a lot of what he thought was bad about the British, and the English in particular. She was a daughter of one of the landed gentry, for instance. She had gone to that most élite of British institutions, the boarding school. And though she wasn't really a snob she occasionally verged on it with her provincial belief and feeling of pride in her run-down little island. But perhaps what annoyed Dempsey most were her continual wise-cracks about America and Americans. Still to be fair, thought Dempsey, this was part of the game that they played with each other and he'd made some pretty wise-cracks in his time. And she did have a great body. He suspected that he did dream about her because he fancied her, or at least his subconscious did. But he tried and put forward other reasons to himself; he thought that it might be because they spent so much time together, or maybe he dreamt about her because she was the absolute antithesis of his dream girl and the only reason that he was waking up all the time was that his dreams were really nightmares and he just didn't realize it. Nevertheless he hoped that one day his dreams about Makepeace would go on for a little longer and then maybe he could find out the truth.

He looked across at his alarm clock. It still read twenty-minutes-past seven. My God you really could dream days in seconds he thought to himself. He shut his eyes and tried to re-enter his dream. But this time he dreamt that a fat fifty year old man with a frightening resemblance to a bulldog was bearing down on top of him, he tried to wake up but he couldn't; Spikings had got him.

June, Kate and Ann were all up and having breakfast when Theodore and George arrived back. Kate was six and little Annie was only four. They both had egg yolk smeared all over their faces but this didn't prevent them from smothering their father in kisses when he produced the flowers from behind his back. He clasped his daughters to him and June rescued the flowers before they were crushed to death in the scrum down. George barked. June put the flowers in a vase on the mantlepiece in the living-room. She glanced down at their wedding photo, she would never have believed that it was possible to maintain such happiness for so long, but here she was, as happy as on her wedding day after twelve years of marriage. She went back into the kitchen where Theodore was trying to remove some of the egg yolk before it set for good. Seeing her enter he gave her a kiss that was almost as eggy as the ones that the girls had given him previously. She brushed him away giggling. George barked again and so Theodore gave him his breakfast.

Breakfast over, teeth brushed, faces washed, lunch boxes packed, Theodore and the girls set off for school, though Theodore was only dropping them off, of course. He did so every morning and June picked them up at three o'clock. They all kissed June goodbye in the doorway and promised to be good in their separate ways. Then skipped off down the path and along the road, hand in hand. June watched them disappear around the corner and then went back inside the house. She thought that she was the luckiest woman alive.

Kate and Ann chatted away all the way to school. They told Theodore how to tell the difference between a toad and a frog, and from frog leapt straight on to school puddings and how revolting they were. Theodore was content just to listen, occasionally umming and arring and prompting them when they lost the thread of their argument. He didn't want to go to work, he wished that he could walk his children to school for ever. He looked up at the bright blue sky and then down at his brilliant children. He thought that he was the luckiest man alive.

Meanwhile Dempsey's dream was progressing well. For a start Spikings had left. Fortunately he hadn't been making sexual advances, as Dempsey had at first supposed, rather he had been trying to collar Dempsey in order to give him a lecture on the difference between English and American morality. In some ways Dempsey reckoned that this might be worse, but fortunately before he'd gone on for too long he had to go off and answer a phone that was ringing. As soon as he'd left, Makepeace entered. Dempsey's eyes stood out like organ stops — she was naked. He'd often dreamt about himself being naked but here, for once, the tables were turned. Perhaps today was the day when the dream would go further. But instead of whispering sweet nothings all Makepeace would say to him was 'Answer the phone'. Dempsey ignored her and strolled casually in her direction but as he did so he heard the phone ringing. He tried to ignore that also, but with each step he took towards Makepeace the phone rang louder. He became annoyed that Spikings had not answered it. He became annoyed with the person phoning him.

How could they be so insensitive? He moved closer to Makepeace but as he did so the ringing of the phone became so loud that it woke him up.

The phone on his bedside table was ringing. He made a grab for it and tipped a glass of water all over his duvet. He swore. He grabbed for the phone again and this time got it without the accompanying shower.

'Yo,' he barked into it, annoyed with whoever had interrupted his dream. He sat up suddenly as he heard Makepeace's voice on the other end. She sounded very different than she had sounded in his dreams. Even when she was ordering Dempsey to answer the phone her voice had been soft and warm, now it was cold and curt. He told himself that he was glad that the dream hadn't gone any further.

'What time is it?' he asked. On hearing her answer he looked across at his alarm clock in disbelief. It still read twenty-minutes-past seven. It was broken. He now knew why she was sounding so cold and curt.

'Harry, I'm sorry. All right. I'm on my way. I overslept.' He put down the phone and rapped his alarm clock. It began to ring very loudly, in turn triggering off a vicious little headache. He rapped it again and it stopped ringing but the damage had been done.

He sat on the edge of his bed for a moment, looking around the room and gathering up courage for his journey to the bathroom. The light from the window had progressed across the floor and was now touching the end of his bed. The weather outside was fabulous but the weather inside was still a little unsettled.

The bathroom was a mess. Dempsey looked at himself in the mirror, he was a mess also but not as bad as the bathroom. The rest of the house was relatively tidy but somehow all the junk seemed to accumulate in the bathroom. He wondered if he were killed in mysterious circumstances on that very day in the line of duty what the boys from forensics would make of his bathroom. There seemed to be clues enough for a hundred murder mysteries accumulated in there. The waste-paper basket where he emptied his pockets was overflowing, there were bottles and pills enough to restock a drugstore, there was even the kitchen sink or something very like it. Everything was there, everything that is apart from his toothbrush. He didn't even bother looking too hard, he just made a mental note to clean up the bathroom as soon as possible. He squeezed the remains of his toothpaste onto his finger and rubbed it ineffectually against his teeth. He lifted up his upper lip and examined them in the mirror. They weren't really the finest teeth imaginable. They weren't dirty but one of the ones right at the back was missing completely, knocked out by a bank robber in New York who was protesting against being arrested, and one of the front ones was slightly chipped, the result of an altercation with a getaway car. At least they had character, thought Dempsey. He made another mental note to buy some more toothpaste from the drugstore on the way home that evening. He liked to use the phrase 'drugstore' as it got up people's noses and reminded him of home.

Teeth cleaned, or at least the taste of last night's party removed, Dempsey splashed some cold water onto his face and tried to exercise a bit of life into his tired eyes. He wanted to have a shower and a shave but there wasn't time, so he slapped on more after-shave than normal to try and compensate for both. He went back into the bedroom and quickly pulled on a white shirt. He took his .44 Magnum off the bedside table where he always kept it when he was in bed and strapped it on. It was always the first thing, after his shirt, that he put on in the mornings, it was like his security blanket. He finished dressing, threw his duvet over his mattress and left. It was now eight thirty and he'd promised Makepeace that he'd be in by eight.

He raced down the stairs and burst out of the front door of the building. The fresh air made him feel like a human being again. But he didn't have time to hang around and marvel at the wonders of the morning. He jogged to where he'd parked his car. He rubbed his hand fondly across the roof. It was a silver Mercedes Cabriolet and it was Dempsey's pride and joy. He'd bought it second-hand but Mercedes were the most reliable cars on the market and Dempsey reckoned that he'd be able to drive his around for another five years and then sell it for more than he had bought it for. He unlocked it and jumped in. He thrust the key into the ignition and twisted it firmly. The starting engine whined but the petrol engine didn't even seem to be turning over. Dempsey tried again but still the car wouldn't start. He thumped the steering wheel in frustration and tried again, this time even the starting motor began to sound unhealthy. He got out and lifted up the bonnet. The engine was still there but God only knew what was wrong with it; God and the Mercedes specialist who thought he was God, or at least charged like him. Dempsey slammed the bonnet down and cursed. He didn't even bother to tinker around with the insides, he didn't have time and besides he wouldn't have known where to start. He gave the back tyre a departing kick and set off down the road looking for a taxi.

It wasn't his day. Every single taxi seemed to be occupied, or if they weren't taken then they didn't have their orange 'for hire' lights on. Dempsey tried to flag a few of the latter down, hoping that their lights had broken or something, but the drivers only gestured at him, either with complex explanations or short commands. He reflected that taxis were a bit like policemen, you could never find one when you needed one. At last, however, one appeared around the corner both empty and with its 'for hire' light on. Dempsey rushed out into the middle of the road and waved at it exaggeratedly, just to make sure that it wouldn't miss him.

It did miss him, but only just and travelling at about forty miles an hour. It was as if it were trying to run him down. Dempsey was furious, he didn't like the idea of being forced to catch a taxi, but he liked the idea of being run down by one even less. He kicked at the side of the taxi as it flew past him. On hearing the thud the taxi driver applied his brakes sharply and the taxi screeched to a halt about two hundred yards up the road. The taxi driver obviously didn't care much about the safety of prospective passengers but he was sensitive about the paintwork on his cab. This was fine by Dempsey. Seeing the cab come to a halt he started to run in its direction hoping to give the driver a piece of his mind. The driver was just getting out of his cab hoping to give Dempsey a piece of his mind, and perhaps even a clip round the ear, when he saw Dempsey, two hundred pounds of irate American policeman approaching him at speed. The cab driver quickly decided that discretion was the better part of valour, he jumped back in his cab and drove off at speed. Two hundred yards further down the road, and travelling at forty miles an hour again, valour gained the upper hand over discretion once more and the departing taxi driver flicked a V-sign back down the road behind him. Dempsey simply smiled at this mock bravado.

Theodore Barret smiled also, revealing his perfect teeth. Kate and Ann smiled back at him, waved from the school steps and then disappeared inside to learn about tadpoles. Theodore stood there for a moment, quietly content. He looked down at his watch. He had just enough time to catch the eight-forty-seven bus. He set off in the direction of the bus stop, whistling softly to himself and continuing to marvel at the almost perfect nature of the day. He rounded the corner and bumped into Dempsey who was also making for the bus stop, though he didn't think that it was quite such a perfect day.

This was the first time that they'd ever seen each other. Though they lived quite close geographically, they inhabited totally different worlds. Dempsey was young and single and though he took his work seriously he also liked to live the high-life on occasion. Theodore was older and married and for him the high life was picking flowers on a Monday morning. But today their two worlds had collided, literally.

Normally Theodore would have said nothing at such an encounter. He would have looked rather embarrassed, tried to apologize with his eyebrows and walked on, head down. This morning, however, he was feeling gay, he knew nothing of the modern connotations of the word, and he wanted to communicate something of his happiness as he felt that he had more than his fair share. He greeted Dempsey with a broad smile and a warm 'Beautiful morning isn't it?'

Normally Dempsey would have replied to such a greeting equally warmly. One of the other things that he hated about the English was what they called 'reserve' but what was really unfriendliness. But this particular morning had been a bad one for him and he was feeling bear-headed, so he just smiled at Theodore in the way that he'd learnt from the British; it was a smile that said 'I really don't want to get into conversation with you and I think that you must be slightly unhinged for addressing me in the first place.' Theodore tried to apologize with his eyebrows and walked on, head down, in the direction of the bus stop. Dempsey followed him, trying not to catch up with him, even though he was a quicker walker.

Catherine Warren watched their approach. Her eyes lit up. The time had come. She ducked down behind the roof's low wall and opened up the briefcase. She began to assemble the rifle. She did so as if it were some kind of ritual. Her hands moved slowly and exactly, and eventually a deadly weapon appeared from what had previously been harmless lumps of metal. She removed a bright brass cartridge with its protruding lead bullet from her pocket and rolled it around on the palm of her hand for a moment. This was the final ingredient. She slid the cartridge into the cold black metal of the rifle and pushed it into firing position with the bolt. The glint of gold disappeared. She only loaded one bullet. One bullet for one person, the simplicity of it pleased her. She peered over the wall down at those waiting at the bus stop. There were ten of them. Ten little niggers, she thought to herself. She attached the telescopic sight and adjusted it for the effect that gravity would have on the bullet over that distance. It wouldn't be much but she liked everything to be exact. She leant the barrel of the rifle on the edge of the wall and scanned across the people at the bus stop through the telescopic sight. She was reminded of a quiz game on television in her youth.

Theodore arrived at the bus stop and Dempsey joined the queue behind him. Dempsey didn't like queueing and he didn't like buses. He sulked. Some of the other people at the bus stop seemed vaguely familiar to him. He'd probably seen them in the local shops and streets, but none of them spoke to him, or each other, even though they had all probably queued for the same bus at the same time for many years. Dempsey remembered why the faces looked so familiar, it was because he'd always seen them queueing here at this bus stop. He used to pass them every morning in his car and think to himself what poor suckers they were. He reminded himself to think that more often. Theodore looked down at his watch. It was another five minutes before the bus was due to arrive. Dempsey looked down at his watch, he didn't know what time the bus was due to arrive but it was a way to pass the time while waiting. He was looking forward to a cup of coffee at the 'shop' and a bit of idle banter with Makepeace.

The crosswire of the telescopic sight on Catherine Warren's rifle rested for a moment in the middle of Theodore Barret's forehead. She smiled at the idea. She imagined the surprised look on his face. She moved the crosswire on and brought it to rest on the middle of Dempsey's forehead. She stopped smiling. She watched as Dempsey brushed a strand of hair away that had fallen in front of his face, it was as if he was preparing the way for the bullet. Just then, out of the corner of her eye Catherine noticed a flash of red. She looked across and saw to her horror that a bus was approaching up the road towards the bus stop. She glanced down at her watch. She hadn't miscalculated, it really was five minutes early. She took aim again but the appearance of the bus had released a sudden pump of adrenalin which made her hand unsteady. She breathed deeply and calmly as she had been taught. Her hand steadied. She re-aimed the rifle.

Dempsey stood still but the girl two places in front of him in the queue, the girl in front of Theodore, stood up on tiptoe to read the number of the bus. As she did so she dropped the magazine from her bag. Theodore bent down to pick it up and so did Dempsey, who was always more sociable when it came to the female of the species. They clashed heads and both stood up smiling at each other stupidly. They both bent down again but as Dempsey was the quicker he got the magazine and avoided the bang on the head. Theodore was less lucky, as he bent down for the second time he received an immense blow on his forehead that threw him backwards as if he were a rag doll. While in flight he could just make out a loud bang but by the time he hit the pavement he was dead.

You only need to have been shot at once to be able to distinguish the sound of gunfire from any other loud noise. Dempsey had been shot at more times than he wished to remember. He reacted like lightning. He dropped to the pavement dragging the girl with the magazine down with him. Then he yelled at the others standing at the bus stop to get down. They just stood there like stupid sheep, not realizing that at any moment they could have been transformed into headless chickens. In one movement Dempsey rolled onto his back, pulled his gun from his shoulder holster and rolled back onto his stomach, his head now protected by the base of the bus stop post. He pointed the gun in the general direction from which he reckoned the shot had been fired. He shouted across at the other commuters who had begun to back away. 'Get down. I'm a police officer.' His tone and the gun seemed to shake them out of their trance. They flattened themselves on the pavement behind him. He waved his gun around from side to side but could see nothing.

There was nothing to see. Catherine had slumped below the level of the wall as soon a she realized that she'd missed, or at least missed her intended target. She was furious with herself. The bus hadn't been early after all. The bus she had seen was a number forty-three and the forty-three turned left a hundred yards before it reached the bus stop at which Dempsey was standing. She had panicked, a cardinal error, and as for bringing only one bullet, she felt sick with herself.

But she recovered quickly. There was no use crying over spilt milk and she was determined to learn by her mistakes. Next time she wouldn't try to be so bloody poetic, attempting to kill him with one bullet, like a werewolf or something. Next time she would bring enough to finish the job. She packed up the rifle as if she was tucking up a loved one and then crawled back across to the fire escape. She climbed over the fence again and disappeared into the bushes where she had left her ordinary clothes. Five minutes later she emerged carrying her briefcase and the carrier-bag with her black clothes in. She strolled back across the park swinging them. She looked like any other petite, thirty year old, brown-haired woman, though now she was looking slightly happier than she'd looked beforehand.

Meanwhile Dempsey, sensing that the main danger had passed, crabbed his way across the pavement to where Theodore was lying. He slapped his hand down in a pool of blood by mistake, splashing himself. There was a small round hole in the middle of Theodore's forehead. There was a huge gaping one at the back. As he looked down at him Dempsey felt that there was something odd about the man. He tried to pinpoint it. He pinpointed it. It was the teeth, Theodore Barret's teeth seemed to be smiling, smiling all by themselves.

TWO

The boys from forensics were on the scene within an hour. They enjoyed a good sniper killing, as it gave them a chance to show off their trigonometry. But, on arrival, it was generally agreed that it was not one of the best. One of the big disappointments was that Theodore was carrying so much identification. They much preferred it when the victim was carrying no identifying papers at all and then they had to work out who he was through medical or dental evidence. Arthur Wilson, who was the chief teeth man, felt that Theodore was carrying so much identification that it had to be a cover, a false identity. He voiced this idea to the others but they didn't go along with it, they'd spoken to some of the other people queueing at the bus stop who had said that Theodore had caught that bus every day for as long as any of them could remember. But Arthur Wilson had his doubts, so he secretly sneaked over to where the now cold

Theodore was lying, pulled off the sheet and took a peek inside his mouth. He was disgusted by what he saw. Not a single filling. He wondered how men like him were expected to do their jobs.

The boys from forensics had managed to find some interesting points, though. There was universal admiration for the quality of the shot. They had no way of knowing that the shot was a complete fluke. In fact, if anybody had told them that it had been a complete fluke, then they would have weighed up the probabilities and laughed them out of court. But it was a fluke shot, of course, though June Barret probably wouldn't have called it that.

The other point that they found interesting concerned the two holes made by the bullet. The entry hole was small and round whereas the exit hole was large and messy. Their interpretation of this was that when the bullet entered his head it was still rifling, i.e. twisting. This gave them some indication of the distance of the assassin from his target, as, after a certain distance, even bullets from highly rifled barrels stopped twisting. From the size of the exit hole they deduced that when the bullet had left Theodore's head it must have been somersaulting, turning end over end. Therefore there was a point within Theodore Barret's brain where the bullet had stopped twisting and started somersaulting. They could hardly wait to take him back and do an autopsy on him.

The local police were quite excited as well. Often the biggest thrill they got in a week was wheel-clamping a Rolls Royce. A sniper killing on their doorstep made them feel very self-important. They were going around asking stupid questions to all and sundry. They'd already asked Dempsey his quota. In fact Dempsey reckoned that he'd got more than his fair share. He could tell that they despised him because he was a member of SI 10, the élite squad, and that they despised him even more because he was an American member of SI 10; to them he had taken a job that should have gone to a Brit. But they were asking him more questions than the others because somehow they thought that he was responsible for this shooting. He didn't think that he was and he told them so in no uncertain terms. He also made a few suggestions which were ignored out of hand. Now he was just leaning against the side of Makepeace's car taking no further part in the proceedings.

Makepeace had arrived about twenty minutes ago; after the local police had reluctantly passed on Dempsey's message to SI 10. It had been good to see her, especially after the coldness of the boys from forensics and the aggressive attitude of the local lads. As Dempsey watched he could see Makepeace trying to wring some information out of them. They didn't appear to be very forthcoming. Dempsey wasn't surprised, after all she was also a member of SI 10 and on top of that she was a woman. Dempsey wondered which was worse, being a woman in England or being an American in England. He decided that they were both as difficult as each other and that was probably why the two of them made such a good team. He looked away from Makepeace and surveyed the rest of the scene.

A policeman was chalking a rough outline around Theodore's body. The drawing completed, two ambulancemen picked the body up, still covered in the sheet, put it on a stretcher and wheeled it into an ambulance. In America they would call the ambulance a meat wagon, thought Dempsey to himself cynically. A small crowd had gathered, mostly shoppers. They were prevented from getting closer by white tapes strung across the street. As soon as these appeared they seemed to attract people like fly paper. They pressed in on the scene as if for warmth, but there was no longer much to see. The chief attraction was probably a policeman sprinkling sand over the sticky gore left on the pavement. He seemed to take great pride in his work, sprinkling on a little sand, waiting for it to be absorbed and then sprinkling on a little more. It looked as if he was trying to save on sand.

Dempsey stood up and walked towards the chalk figure outlined on the pavement. He stood over it for a moment. It wasn't a very good likeness. He tilted his head to one side. In the blue flashing lights of the ambulances and police cars it looked as if it was trying to dance. A press photographer took a photograph of the dancing man. Dempsey walked back to the car. He felt curiously removed from his surroundings and the morning's events. There was a line of poetry that fitted his mood but he couldn't think of it. He looked across at Makepeace. She seemed to be doing better than before, she was writing things down in her notebook.

Dempsey's fellow queuers were being treated for shock. A few had been taken away in ambulances but most had been simply wrapped in blankets and administered with that wonder drug, hot sweet tea. Their skin was pale and their expressions glazed, some of them were still trembling. Dempsey felt a sudden and illogical loathing for them; not because they were suffering from shock; there was nothing wrong with suffering from shock when you had witnessed what they had just witnessed, in fact there was probably something wrong with you if you didn't suffer from shock, but he felt loathing for them because he couldn't help feeling that they were shocked only because they realized that they could have been that crude chalk outline peppered with the policeman's sand. The girl who had dropped the magazine and whom Dempsey had dragged to the floor seemed to have been the worst affected, though it was the dragging down itself that had shocked her most. Dempsey couldn't feel too sorry for her either, the magazine that she'd dropped had been *True Life Romance*. It was a strange thing to owe one's life to.

Suddenly one of the forensic boys called from the top of the warehouse opposite. He'd found the spent cartridge. He held it aloft and those on the street waved up to him in congratulation. For them it seemed to be no more than a treasure hunt. Another succeeded in digging out the bullet from the low brick wall in which it had become embedded. The others clustered round to look at it. It was just a deformed lump of lead but they took it in turns to weigh it in their hands. It was generally agreed that it was a bullet from a high calibre rifle.

Dempsey watched them go about their business. He decided that he didn't like them. In fact after the morning's events he didn't really like anyone much. If his own mother had turned up he would probably have decided that he didn't like her. But the particular reason that he didn't like the boys from forensics at the moment was that he objected to their attitude. They treated everything as if it were a crossword puzzle or a quiz game or something. For them the bullet was more important than the human being that it had passed through. Possessions were more important than emotions. All that was interesting from their point of view was the scientific side of things. The concept of people very seldom seemed to occur to them. Perhaps that was the way you had to be in order to deal daily with sights like the back of Theodore Barret's head and still remain sane. But at this point in time, and in his particular state of mind, Dempsey rather doubted that they were human, even though he'd heard that they displayed a great sense of humour in the autopsy room.

He took out a cigar, lit it and inhaled deeply. Arthur Wilson, the teeth specialist, came up to him to tell him something particularly gruesome that might have happened inside Theodore's brain. Dempsey told him that he didn't want to know and so Arthur Wilson told him something particularly gruesome that could happen to a person's insides if they smoked. Dempsey told him something particularly gruesome that could happen to a person's outsides if they talked too much. Arthur Wilson left.

Dempsey took another deep drag on his cigar. In doing so he noticed that he had blood on his hands. He examined it. There was blood on his shirt as well. He swore. The shirt had been clean on that morning and he didn't know whether he had another clean one. Suddenly he stopped himself. He wondered if he was becoming like the boys in forensics. Had he too become so hardened to such things that when he was splashed by the blood of a dying man all that he could worry about was his laundry bill? He thought the question over. He decided that it wasn't that he had become callous, it was just that he was pissed off, pissed off with everything.

Makepeace made her way in his direction. She smiled at him and he began to feel slightly less pissed off. 'They through with me?' he asked.

She nodded and fixed him with her perfect blue

eyes, there was a glint of humour in them. 'Nice start to the day,' she said. Dempsey smiled at her. He liked their conversation together. There was always an element of challenge, competition and also, deep down, a great deal of warmth, though they were probably the only two who could recognize it.

'Yeh, business is picking up, eh?' he replied.

'See anything?'

'A big close-up of the sidewalk.'

Makepeace recognized that Dempsey was in one of his more awkward moods, so she ignored his flippancy and continued her questioning. She decided that she'd try and teach him to say pavement, rather than sidewalk, at some later date.

'How many shots?'

'One,' snapped Dempsey 'Wasn't that enough?' Her questions were beginning to annoy him, she was sounding too like the local police. For a brief moment he was given an insight into how it felt to be on the other end of an interrogation.

Makepeace was quite taken aback by his sudden aggression. There was absolutely no cause for him to be so short with her. If their roles had been reversed and she had been the one standing in the bus queue, then he would have asked her exactly the same questions. But, though she was tempted, she refrained from replying to Dempsey's question by suggesting that one shot hadn't been enough. She reckoned that even Dempsey had a right to behave a little strangely after the person standing next to him in the bus queue had had their brains blown out. It wasn't an everyday occurrence, even for a policeman. In fact, in some ways, she felt that it was quite a good sign that he could be affected by such an event. She looked up at the roof of the warehouse from which the forensics man had waved. It was a lovely day. It didn't seem fair to her that anyone should die on such a day, let alone anyone have their brains blown out at a bus stop.

Dempsey recovered his cool, though, like Makepeace, he was quite glad that he'd lost it. He was glad that he still had the capacity to be upset by man's violence and inhumanity even after so many years of witnessing it at such close quarters. But, having recognized this in himself, he quickly reverted to type; laid-back and cynical.

'What do we know about the stiff?' he asked Makepeace, disturbing her from her musings. She consulted her notebook and relayed the small amount of information that she had managed to gather from the local police.

'Theo Barret. Aged thirty-eight. Married — two children.' She closed the notebook. That was all. That was his life. 'Shall we go talk to his wife?' she asked and then, realizing her mistake, added 'Or should I say the widow?'

'Well I'd like to wash-up first,' said Dempsey, holding out his hand to show the dried blood. Makepeace looked at him with distaste.

'I think you'd better. Mrs Barret might not appreciate you turning up with Mr Barret's blood all over your hands. I'll give you a lift if you like.' Makepeace opened her car door in order to climb in but Dempsey pulled her back.

'It's OK I live just round the block and I'd prefer to walk it.'

'You're not inviting me round then?' she asked hopefully.

'Some other time. I won't be long. I just want to wash this stuff off and change my shirt.'

'OK.'

'Perhaps you could try and find out a bit more about this Basset guy.'

'Barret guy,' corrected Makepeace.

'Barret guy. Whether there were any rumours or gossip about him or anything like that.'

'OK I'll have a go, but I'd have difficulty getting the name of the Queen of England out of this lot.'

'Well don't worry, I may be American, but I know the answer to that one already. See ya later.'

'Bye.'

Dempsey walked back to his flat slowly, immersed in thought. He was trying to make sense of things. He was a cop who seemed to attract crime. Some cops might have thought that that was a good thing, you didn't have to go out looking for it, but Dempsey wasn't one of those cops. He wanted to keep his work and private life as separate as possible. He wanted to forget about crime when he wasn't on a case. He wanted to lead a perfectly normal life, but he couldn't. Wherever he went, whatever he did, whatever time he did it, crime seemed to follow him.

That morning he felt that things had reached quite ludicrous proportions. Nothing could have been more banal or innocuous than queueing for a bus on a Monday morning and yet, what had happened, but the man standing next to him had been murdered by a professional killer. Dempsey wondered whether perhaps everyone led lives like his nowadays. Perhaps crime was so prevalent that it was impossible to avoid it. Everyone encountered it every day. He dropped the idea. He felt fatalistic. He felt that there was no explaining it; he just attracted crime like shit attracts flies and that was the end of it.

He passed his Mercedes again and gave it another

hefty kick. He felt that it was the car's fault. He would have read all about this thing in the papers if the bloody car hadn't broken down, so much for German engineering. He entered his flat, gently removed his gun and laid it on his bed. He tore off his shirt and threw it at an empty suitcase which was spewing its contents all over the bedroom floor. He washed the blood off in the bathroom. It came off with greater ease than he'd expected. He took a clean shirt out of his chest-of-drawers. It was his last one. He cursed, as it meant that he'd have to do his washing that evening.

He returned to the scene of the crime some fifteen minutes later. He still felt dirty. Makepeace looked squeaky clean as ever. She was leaning against the bonnet of her Jaguar watching his approach.

'Find out anything more?' he asked cheerfully, trying to sound as if he felt he was on top of the world. Makepeace shook her head.

'Nothing important. Just that his two kids were called Kate and Ann.'

'Might they have had any reason to kill their father?'

'I doubt it. They were six and four.' Dempsey looked sheepish. 'He might have been behind on the pocket money payments,' he suggested. Makepeace ignored him.

'Shall we go?' She held the passenger door open for Dempsey.

'Have you got the address?'

'Well if I hadn't we wouldn't know where to go to would we?'

'My point exactly,' said Dempsey smugly.

'Well I have, now get in.' She pushed Dempsey into the car and climbed into the driver's seat herself. She thrust the key into the ignition and was about to turn it when Dempsey interrupted her.

'Let's make tracks then Watson,' he said rather fatuously.

Makepeace took the keys out of the ignition and stared at him angrily. He didn't seem to know what he'd done wrong. So Makepeace told him. 'This is my car.' Her voice was harsh but Dempsey could tell that she was also rather relishing her position. 'Your marvellous piece of highly-tuned German sculpture wouldn't start this morning, if you remember. So if we're going to drive around in my car all day, which may not be as expensive as yours but at least it goes, then you're going to have to be the side-kick.'

Dempsey weighed up the situation.

'OK, hit the gas then, Holmes.'

Theodore Barret's address was forty-three New Mill Avenue. It was only a couple of hundreds yards from where he died; easily within rifle range. It was so close that Dempsey and Makepeace didn't really need to drive there, it would probably have been just as quick to walk. When they arrived there was still a police panda car parked outside. Obviously the bringers of the bad news were still inside. They decided that they would have to wait until the patrolmen left. They had to wait for quite a while. Dempsey reflected that in Ancient Greece the bringers of bad news were often beheaded, while in England they were sometimes given a cup of tea. He stared fixedly at the Barrets' front door willing the policemen inside to leave. Makepeace stared fixedly at him. Already there were many things that puzzled her about the morning's happenings. She knew that trouble followed Dempsey around as she was normally there when it caught up with him. Crime seemed to be attracted to him like bees to honey. Her choice of phrase was more delicate than Dempsey's. But a full blown, professional-looking assassination happening to a man standing next to Dempsey in the bus queue, that seemed to be too much to be explained away by any stupid smile. Sure, Miss Marple always, very fortunately, just happened to be at the scene of gruesome murders in the Vicarage Garden, but Miss Marple had Agatha Christie to type out her life for her. Makepeace didn't believe in the celestial typewriter. She felt sure that Dempsey must be more than just an innocent by-stander. She hoped that he wasn't holding anything back from her.

Her thoughts were interrupted by a nudge from Dempsey. The policeman had emerged from the house. Dempsey and Makepeace watched them get into their panda and drive off, neither envied them the task they had just performed; they had both served their time in uniform also. They gave Mrs Barret five minutes. Not that it was time enough to recover from the news of the loss of her husband. It just seemed the polite thing to do.

Makepeace rang the bell. The door chime had a jarringly happy note. June Barret made her way towards the front door. They could make out her outline through the frosted glass as she approached. Her movements were those of an old woman. But when she opened the door they could see that she was only in her late thirties. She stared up at them blankly. Her eyes were ringed with red and seemed to have guttered into her face. The effect was height-ened by the paleness of her skin. She was the very opposite of the woman who had kissed her family good-bye a couple of hours earlier. Looking at her pitiful state, Makepeace decided that it might be best if she did the talking.

'Hello Mrs Barret, my name's Harriet Makepeace ...' she showed Mrs Barret her card. '... and this is James Dempsey.' She presented him like a newly acquired husband. 'We're police officers and we've. ...'

'I know,' interrupted Mrs Barret, clinging to the door frame for support. 'They've told me already.'

Makepeace realized that she thought that they'd come to inform her of the death of her husband again. She wished that she could just go and leave this woman to her private sorrow. The poor woman obviously hadn't taken the death of her husband well. She looked as if her whole world and reason for living had suddenly been taken from her. But, unfortunately, they had a job to do and, though it seemed cruel at the time, it might prevent further grief.

'We just want to ask you a few questions,' explained Makepeace.

'Questions?' repeated Mrs Barret as if she had no idea what the word meant.

'About your husband.'

Mrs Barret stared at them. She knew what the word 'husband' meant. What she didn't know was what she'd do without him. She looked again at the two strangers standing in the doorway. They looked as if they wanted to come in. She didn't know why and she didn't care why. She moved aside to let them in.

As they entered George wagged his tail in anticipation. He didn't know that Mrs Barret would be forced to put him down, now Theodore was dead. Dempsey liked dogs, but this didn't seem to be the time or the place to get down on his hands and knees and play. They brushed past George into the living-room; he followed. It had been quite an exciting day for him, very seldom did they have so many visitors.

Mrs Barret fell into an armchair. Dempsey and Makepeace perched uneasily on the edge of the sofa opposite her. They had both done this kind of questioning many times before but it still made them nervous. Mrs Barret started crying uncontrollably. They looked elsewhere.

The living-room was very homely. It was full of the bric-à-brac that the two of them had collected over the twelve years of their marriage. But it wasn't cluttered. Each item had its allotted position and was dusted regularly. Theodore's television slippers lay underneath the rented set and on the small table next to his television chair was placed his pipe and all the materials he used for cleaning it. Makepeace wondered how long it would be before Mrs Barret would be brave enough to throw all this stuff out. She looked across at her and began to think that perhaps she never would. Perhaps, like a character in a Dickens novel, she would refuse to accept his death and would maintain the room as a shrine to his memory. Mrs Barret stopped crying and Dempsey decided that now was the time to begin the interrogation before they lost her completely.

He took a deep breath and began. 'Mrs Barret did your husband ...'

Mrs Barret interrupted him. 'Did he die quickly?'

'Instantaneous, ma'am,' replied Dempsey trying to sound as sorrowful as possible.

'No pain?'

'No, he can't have felt a thing.' Dempsey gave the reply that he knew was expected of him. It was the truth, of course. For a tiny fraction of a second Theodore would have felt a sharp pain on his forehead but he was dead long before it could have become agonizing or before he could let out a scream. Still, Dempsey couldn't help feeling that if he were going to die he'd like to know about it. Even if he couldn't manage anything epigrammatic for his last words, he'd at least like a few good last thoughts. But it seemed to comfort relatives to be told that their loved ones died instantly and felt no pain.

Mrs Barret had started crying again. It was a pitiful sight but, at least, she hadn't become violent as some of them did. Makepeace had known the recently bereaved to try and murder the police officers who turned up to question them. It was a bit like a Greek myth she thought to herself. She'd had a classical education.

Suddenly Mrs Barret returned to the world of the living again. There'd been something puzzling her. She fixed Dempsey with her blood-shot eyes.

'How do you know?' she asked aggressively.

Demsey had no idea what she was getting at. 'How do I know what?'

'How do you know that he died instantly and suffered no pain?' she replied. Her eyes had grown fierce with accusation.

'Well I was there when he died,' he explained.

'You were there?' she sounded amazed. She too, even in the depth of her grief, recognized his presence as a strange coincidence.

'Right next to him,' continued Dempsey 'As close to him as I am to you now. Closer.'

Mrs Barret's eyes wavered for a moment, as if on the brink of some kind of trance. The physicality of the idea was too much for her. She felt that she was the one who should have been that close to him when he died. She'd lived with him so happily for so long and now the police came knocking on her door to tell her that he was dead. How did she even know that they were telling the truth? Why should she believe them? Why had it happened? Why was it him? Why was it her? The thoughts became one word. 'Why?'

She asked it quietly but that didn't make it any easier to answer. It was an impossible question. Neither Dempsey nor Makepeace had an answer to it. The only person who might have found one was Theodore and he was keeping mum.

'Why?' she asked again, her voice now loud and bitter. 'Why was it him and not you?'

Dempsey looked at her. The question was addressed to him. It had become more defined but it was still impossible to answer. It was a question that had been welling up inside him also. He didn't believe that there was an answer. He was glad that it had been Theodore Barret and not James Dempsey, but another day it could equally well be the other way round; the question would be asked again and there still wouldn't be an answer. Nevertheless, he wished that he could give an answer that would help Mrs Barret there and then.

Makepeace came to his rescue. She knew what Mrs Barret had meant by her question and, like Dempsey, she also knew that there wasn't an answer. So, like a good politician, she answered a different question.

'That's what we intend to find out,' she said, taking out her notebook and licking her pencil in order to try and bring the conversation back down to the physical and factual.

'What was he doing there at that time of the morning?' she asked. She held her pencil poised over her pad waiting to take down Mrs Barret's reply. Mrs Barret tried to make sense of the question and, as its impact filtered through, something resembling a smile passed across her face. She wondered what they were trying to get at. They thought that there was something unusual in him being there at that time in the morning. It was comic but she couldn't bring herself to laugh. Theodore had queued up at that bus stop every working day for the past twelve years, apart from the day that she had given birth to Kate that is. Did they think that he was some kind of secret agent? Did they think that there was some kind of motive behind his killing? Did they think that if there was a motive behind his killing, that she would feel it was some consolation? She could no longer weep. She was past that stage.

Her mind and eyes both wandered. On the wall there were some drawings done in wax crayon and painted over with powder paints. The paint didn't soak in where the paper had been waxed. She wondered how she'd break the news to Kate and Ann. She wondered how they'd take it, or whether they would be able even to understand it. She didn't care who had killed him. She had no desire for revenge. All that she wanted was her husband back. She looked along the mantlepiece. Theodore smiled at her from their wedding photo. She held his arm. What a day that had been. She'd hoped that they would live happily ever after.

Dempsey and Makepeace followed her gaze. They were both fast coming to the same conclusion. No one could possibly have wanted Theodore Barret dead, or at least no one in their right mind. Something had gone wrong somewhere. Someone had made a mistake, a fatal mistake. They'd both seen fronts before, false identities; multi-millionaire drug dealers posing as unemployed labourers and living in broken down council housing, charming old men with stamp collections turning out to be child molesters, loving husbands of happy families turning out to be malicious rapists. But this, no this was real life.

June continued to stare at the wedding photograph on the mantelpiece. Dempsey looked at it too. The man in the photograph was quite a bit younger than the one that he had seen lying on the pavement. He hadn't aged badly, but it was noticeable. The only thing that hadn't changed were his teeth, all that was different about the smile was that in the photograph he had something to smile about. George dropped a large and bloody bone onto Dempsey's shoes. It made him jump. George looked up at him eagerly but Dempsey wasn't hungry, all he wanted to do was to get out of there. He was feeling suddenly rather sick.

June's gaze moved from the wedding photograph to the four cards that stood awkwardly in line beside it. 'Thursday was our anniversary ..,' she said to no one in particular. She paused to wipe away the snot that trickled from her nose. 'Theodore bought me a negligee ... it was only two sizes too small ...' her eyes clouded over for a moment and then cleared again. 'Twelve years married, two children and he still thinks that I'm the same size.' If Theodore had been alive it would have been a joke; as it was comedy had turned into tragedy.

Makepeace could see that they were losing her. She was beginning to enter a world of remembrances, unable to face reality. Cruel though it seemed, they had to ask her a few questions before they could allow her to suffer her grief in private.

'Did he have any enemies?' Makepeace asked the

question directly and in a matter of fact tone so that Mrs Barret *had* to answer her.

'Enemies?' repeated June 'You mean people who would want to kill him?' Makepeace nodded, ignoring the note of incredulity in Mrs Barret's voice.

June looked across at Makepeace, the only emotion now visible in her eyes was one of the deepest sadness.

'Miss Makepeace,' she asked softly 'who would want to kill a man like Theodore? He was a small wheel in a large life insurance company. He was a husband and a father. No more than that.'

Makepeace again could provide no answer for her question. Dempsey toyed briefly with the idea of some personal life insurance policy scam. He looked across at the wedding photograph again. Theodore smiled on. Dempsey dropped the idea. But Mrs Barret's question still hung in the air and Makepeace was beginning to look uneasy under the scrutiny of those sad red eyes. It was Dempsey's turn to come to the rescue. He did so by becoming a policeman again. 'Did he have any phone calls . . . or letters that upset him . . . business problems or problems of any other kind?'

But his question remained unanswered also. They'd lost her. She had no time for their stupid questions any more. Her eyes settled on the flowers that Theodore had picked that morning. She remembered the joy that she had felt when he had given them to the girls such a short time ago. She pointed them out to her guests. 'See those? He picked those this morning before he took the girls off to school.'

They looked across at the flowers. They dandelions and the cow parsley were already wilting and so was the purple one whose name they didn't know. Only the forget-me-nots looked as if they would last out the day.

Chapter
THREE

The first five minutes of the journey back to the 'shop' they spent in total silence. They'd left Mrs Barret alone in the house pawing over old photograph albums. They'd phoned the social services who were sending someone round but they knew that the only person who would really do her some good would be someone skilled in resurrection. The poor woman still had to tell her children what had happened and she might even have to go down to the mortuary to identify him. It had been a depressing morning all round.

Makepeace was the first to break the silence. 'What are you thinking?'

Dempsey stared straight ahead, his eyes focused on the horizon. 'Poor bloody woman, that's what I was thinking.'

'But who do you think could have done it?'

Dempsey shrugged. 'God knows. I mean, either he led the most amazing and complete double-life that

I've ever seen or he was mistaken for someone else. Maybe it was the work of some nut. Perhaps the milkman is a psycho and Mr Barret owed him for a quart of cream, so he decided to blow him away instead.'

'Perhaps it was an accident,' added Makepeace thoughtfully.

Dempsey looked across at her in disbelief. 'What a shot like that with a high calibre rifle? You've got to be kidding.'

'Funnier things have happened.'

'Oh yeah, well tell me about them then. I want to die laughing.'

The rest of the journey back to the 'shop' they spent in total silence.

When they got in they received confirmation that the case was officially theirs. The local police had wanted it but those in high places had decided that, if there was a sniper running around loose in London, then it would be safer and quicker if SI 10 dealt with it. Dempsey imagined the faces of the local boys when they'd been told that. He hoped that he wouldn't bump into them again before they'd had a chance to cool down.

Dempsey and Makepeace were glad that they'd got the case, but the only trouble now was that there was nothing to go on. There wasn't even a possible motive to work back from. All they had was a small chunk of lead and a brass cartridge. They awaited the ballistics report eagerly, but they held out little hope that anything would come of it.

It seemed to be a long time coming. Dempsey killed time by trying to tidy up his desk and Makepeace whiled away the minutes giving Sergeants Johnson and Matthey her advice about a corruption case they were working on. But eventually both she and

Dempsey ended up drinking coffee and looking at their watches as usual.

At last, after what seemed like an age, but was, in fact, only two hours, Watson arrived with the report. He had orders to show it to Spikings first, so they followed him into Spikings' office. Spikings glanced through it and read out the relevant sections to them. 'Um ... the bullet dug out of the wall and the ejected shell were compatible'. He searched through the report for more information, '... they were both 7.62mm Parker Hale.' He ran his fat thumb down the page. 'Full metal case ... lead alloy jacketed bullet ... soft nose, right hand twist ... weighted about 191.6 grammes.' He closed up the folder and chucked it on the desk in front of Makepeace. She wondered briefly how important it was to know the weight of the bullet to the nearest tenth of a gramme.

'Telescopic sight?' asked Dempsey as a joke. Spikings didn't get it. 'Even the boys from forensics can't tell that from a bullet,' he answered earnestly, 'But I think it must have been.'

'Still a helluva shot, even with a telescopic sight.' Dempsey couldn't help betraying a hint of admiration for the skill of the assassin, but then he remembered the teeth and it quickly disappeared. 'No messages, no calls?' he asked in an attempt to forget about the teeth. The question intrigued Spikings.

'Why? Should there be?' he probed. But, before Dempsey could answer, Makepeace butted in and explained the reason for Dempsey's question.

'Dempsey thinks that some nut shot Barret.' Her tone was disparaging. She didn't go along with Dempsey's theory and she didn't try and hide the fact.

Dempsey threw his arms up in the air to mock

despair. 'Oh come on. You don't think that it was some fruitcake?' He turned to her in disbelief. 'Come on why else would some nice, thirty-eight year old, family man get iced?' He stood up and placed his face close to hers. 'Nuts,' he said as if that was the be-all and end-all of it.

He straightened up and began pacing up and down the room. He could tell that both Spikings and Makepeace thought that he was hiding something. He felt their probing eyes on the back of his neck. Their attitude annoyed him. It was the British attitude. There always had to be calm logical motives for them. They worked under the shadow of the tradition of the gentleman murderer who is trapped by the magnifying glass and clever use of the notebook and who, when caught, congratulates Scotland Yard on their ingenuity.

He was about to point out to them what things were really like when Spikings interrupted. His interruption served only to reinforce Dempsey's opinions. 'Dempsey, now hang about.' He tried to halt Dempsey's pacing, by suddenly standing, but Dempsey paced on. 'This isn't Dallas . . . this is dull old London. Remember?' Dempsey snarled at him. He didn't need, or want, the geography lesson. 'We don't have many snipers here. Football hooligans . . . a tower . . . a queen . . . some warm beer . . . but not many snipers.'

Dempsey stopped pacing and looked Spikings straight in the eye. 'Nuts' he reiterated, though the way he said it to Spikings it had become rather ambiguous. He turned to Makepeace, 'Nuts,' he said again, 'get on your computer and get peddling.'

Makepeace gave him a mock salute and re-entered the central office to get a print-out of the names they always got a print-out of when they had no clues.

Spikings flopped his large bulk back down into his chair. He felt that they were a great team, the three of them, but he couldn't for the life of him work out why. Dempsey stood at the window staring out into the distance. The telephone rang and Spikings snatched it up in his fat fist. It was SI 10 policy not to speak on the phone until spoken to. A ploy to try and avoid practical jokers and nuts getting hold of their number. So Spikings listened while the voice on the other end spoke.

'Who's this?' he asked removing the phone slightly from his ear and looking into the mouthpiece as if the caller were lurking in there. Dempsey turned away from the window and stood watching Spikings. There had been something strange about the way he'd asked the question. 'Hang on.' He placed his hand over the mouthpiece and beckoned to Dempsey.

'What?' asked Dempsey apprehensively.

'It's for you.' Spikings handed him the phone. Dempsey looked at the phone and then at him. Spikings was obviously very keen to find out who was on the other end.

He placed the phone to his ear and tried to muster as much enthusiasm as he could manage. 'Yo — Dempsey.'

For a few seconds there was no reply and then suddenly Dempsey's worst fears were realized. The voice that spoke to him was a woman's voice. She was whispering but Dempsey could hear every word that she said as each was individually and labouriously enunciated. It was the voice of a madwoman. It was Catherine Warren's voice.

'It should've been *you*, Dempsey,' whispered the voice. 'It should've been you with the bullet through the head.'

A sudden feeling of cold swept through Dempsey's body. Makepeace entered and she saw the feeling flash across his eyes. She knew at once what was happening. She knew that Dempsey had proved to be right, that it was a nut after all and that was who was on the phone. Threats they could both of them normally handle; gangland thugs offering them concrete sleeping bags, terrorists offering to decrease the size of their families. It was threats from lunatics that were frightening. Even thugs and terrorists had reasons for what they did, no matter how unreasonable they might seem. Lunatics, however, often had no reason, no logical reason, and that's what made them both dangerous and frightening. Policework relied on logic, the ability to follow up leads, discern motives, but when dealing with a deranged mind this became altogether more difficult.

Spikings also noticed the change come over Dempsey and, though he didn't read into it all that Makepeace did, he recognized that it was no ordinary phonecall. He switched it over to broadcast and yelled out to Watson, who was sitting at his desk in the central office. 'Watson, trace this call. Yellow line.'

Dempsey steadied himself. He could tell already that he wasn't going to enjoy this telephone conversation but he also knew that he had to string it out for as long as possible in order to give Watson a good chance of tracing it. He decided on the deafness routine. He thought that it might work especially as the woman was disguising her voice by whispering. It might also make her speak up and give a truer indication of her own voice, or so he thought. 'Er — could you speak up?' he said quietly, hoping that she might think that the line was bad and that she *had* to speak up.

But he could tell at once that she wasn't going to fall for it. She was definitely mad but unfortunately she didn't seem to be stupid. A mocking element entered her voice. 'This morning at the bus stop,' she whispered.

'What about it?' Dempsey asked the question as if he, like Theodore Barret, had caught the bus every day of his life and that that Monday morning had been just like any other Monday morning.

The voice grew harsher, but no louder. 'It should have been *your* brain that that bullet blew out.'

Dempsey switched to the dumb American routine. 'So what are you telling me?'

Catherine Warren's voice grew harsher still. She didn't like Dempsey and she didn't like Dempsey playing games with her. 'I'm telling you. *You're* next. You're going to have to die Dempsey.' She put the phone down, pleased that she had now made up for her little mistake of the morning.

Dempsey put his phone down also. He looked less pleased. He felt exactly the same way about lunatics as Makepeace did. He hated them and he hated them even more when it turned out that they were trying to kill him. He glanced across at Makepeace. She was staring intently at the telephone broadcast speaker. It still buzzed audibly. Spikings lent across and switched it off, breaking Makepeace's chain of thought.

Dempsey was the first to break the silence. 'Did I say fruitcake? I underestimated.'

'You recognize the voice?' asked Spikings.

Dempsey snarled at him. 'Yes — it was my mother. Course not.' Dempsey had had enough of stupid questions for one day. But he sensed that both Spikings and Makepeace wanted some kind of further explanation. He tried to give them one. 'Some kook got my number out of the phone book. I don't know.'

But the other two patently felt that he did know, or at least knew more than he was telling. Dempsey sat down, trying to ignore their stares, but he could tell that they were prepared to wait. He began to feel uneasy. 'What the hell are you looking at?' he asked, turning to out-face their stares. 'I've never heard that voice before.'

'Yes well that might be true,' persisted Spikings, 'but you can't just palm us off with rubbish like "some kook got my number out of the phone book" we're not idiots you know. A. you're not in the phone book and B. neither is SI10. We're not like Jim Rockford, we don't have an advert in the Yellow Pages.'

Dempsey took a deep breath to try and calm himself down a fraction. 'I know. I know. I'm sorry. It was just something I said off the top of my head.'

'Well, if you don't want to lose the top of your head, then you'd better level with us now,' chipped in Makepeace.

'Oh come on, give me a break,' implored Dempsey. 'I am levelling with you. I swear to God that I've never heard that voice before.'

Makepeace looked him straight in the eye as he said it. She was inclined to believe him. She knew that he was quite prone to lying when he saw things in terms of personal vendettas and especially when these personal vendettas concerned women. But he'd had a bad day and bad days are difficult days on which to tell lies and get away with it. Besides, her intuition told her that he didn't recognize the voice, though whether he'd ever heard it before was a different matter. She looked across at Spikings who seemed to be spoiling for a show-down and decided that

54

Dempsey might be more communicative with her if she got Spikings off his back.

'Look just because it's a woman's voice on the phone doesn't mean that she did the shooting. There could be two of them. Or more.'

'Might be,' mumbled Spikings, still more interested in giving Dempsey a bit of a tongue-lashing.

'Perhaps it was the wife of someone we've put away,' persisted Makepeace.

She'd grabbed his attention. He liked her suggestion. 'That's worth checking on.'

The attention off him, Dempsey walked to the window and looked out. The sky was clouding over and the wind was building up. He didn't listen to their conversation. The image of Mrs Barret returned to him, flicking through photographs of her husband. It was all that she had left of him. Dempsey felt as if he were responsible. So many minute and unaccountable events had led up to the bullet going through Theodore Barret's brain and not his. Things could have turned out so many different ways, so many far happier ways. But the fact was, they hadn't.

Dempsey noticed that the room had fallen silent. He turned to Spikings and Makepeace and tried to explain something of his thoughts. 'Some guy got iced 'cos of me. I got a real sick feeling inside.'

It hadn't come out as he'd expected to and only went a tiny way towards explaining how he was feeling. But it felt good to admit it and not keep it bottled up inside. He'd said it simply and directly and now could go back to being a policeman again. He left the office with Spikings' and Makepeace's eyes still on him. Spikings closed the door behind him.

For the rest of the day Dempsey had an uneasy feeling that Makepeace was mothering him. He was quite enjoying it actually. He just hoped that it hadn't been Spikings' idea. The two of them still didn't have anything much to do. The phonecall had been far too short to be traced. They had scanned through the computer print-out of homicidal maniacs on the loose but most had turned out to be axe-wielders rather than expert snipers. Neither of them were particularly surprised. Now all that they could do was to wait.

Makepeace approached carrying two cups of coffee and a plate of gingernuts, Dempsey's favourites. Dempsey took his boots off the desk. She handed him his coffee and watched him thoughtfully as he sipped it. Dempsey noticed her expression. 'I know what you're thinking Harry,' he said defensively.

'It's this plate glass forehead of mine.'

Dempsey now felt sure that Spikings had told her to try and cheer him up. He continued with the mind reading. 'You may find this hard to believe . . . but I'm actually on good terms with all of my ex girlfriends.'

'All of them?' She asked the question as if it were impossible to know that many people, let alone be on good terms with them all.

Dempsey ignored her tone of voice. 'Yes, all. Well if I wasn't, it wouldn't be my head that they were trying to blow off.'

Makepeace ignored the sexual allusion. 'What about the ones that never made it as girlfriends — ships in the night?'

Dempsey laughed at the coyness of her phrase. 'Ships in the night' sounded Victorian. In America 'ships in the night' were called quickies, it sounded like some kind of fast food but it was infinitely more applicable than Makepeace's contrived nautical phrase. Dempsey decided to try and shake her out her romantic sensibilities. He shook his head wisely. 'There are just too many evil germs around these days for that game any more.'

Makepeace didn't bat an eyelid. She continued with her gentle interrogation. 'Chances are that it's someone you know though isn't it?'

Dempsey thought for a moment. 'Well there is one.' He paused for a moment and then seemed to discount it. 'Nah ... nah.' He waved the thought away as if it were a smell.

But Makepeace knew him too well. If he thought he'd remembered who it was, he might well decide to go for her on his own. She wasn't about to let him do that. 'Who?' she pressed.

Dempsey shook his head. 'No it was just an idea. It's all too implausible.'

But Makepeace was hooked now and Dempsey knew it. She had to find out who he was thinking of. 'Who is it?' she demanded.

Dempsey relented. 'Well there's only one broad I know who can shoot like that.' He looked into her eyes. 'And might have cause.'

Makepeace wasn't amused. He'd meant her. She should have known from his serious tone of voice that he was playing one of his games. But she didn't show him how unfunny she thought it was, she just smiled at him sweetly. Spikings had told her to try and get something out of him by mothering him.

Makepeace continued with the mothering policy for a little longer but her heart wasn't really in it. She sensed that Dempsey knew that Spikings had put her up to it and was toying with her. Besides she felt that Spikings was wrong. She believed that Dempsey really didn't know anything more about the woman's voice than they did. On top of this he seemed to have reverted back to his normal self. Makepeace pitied his real mother.

Makepeace was right, Dempsey did feel his normal self again. Admitting that he hadn't felt his normal self had done him no end of good. He was a trifle disappointed that Makepeace had given up her mothering role though, but, on second thoughts, perhaps it was for the best; he had rather missed their snappy dialogues.

There wasn't much chance for them that afternoon though, as Spikings made Dempsey listen to the tape-recording of the voice all afternoon. (All calls to SI 10 were recorded just in case of such an occurrence.) Dempsey listened to the tape until he thought that he was going mad too. But this feeling of madness was really the only result, and not a very positive one. The woman was both whispering and disguising her voice. Dempsey felt that it could have been anyone. It was a rather frightening thought. Dempsey contemplated becoming a misogynist. He looked across at Makepeace and contemplated something else.

Spikings let Dempsey go half an hour early, which for Spikings was an act of unbridled generosity. Dempsey could tell that Spikings thought so also. Dempsey almost felt touched, until he found out that he wouldn't let anyone else off early to give him a lift home. Makepeace offered to but Spikings had her phoning around lunatic asylums asking for recently escaped female snipers. She was sure that it wouldn't lead to anything but Spikings insisted. She told Dempsey that she would phone him later.

Dempsey didn't relish the idea of using London

Transport again but he decided that he ought to, just to make sure that he didn't develop a phobia about it. Fortunately he didn't have to queue too long at the bus stop before his bus arrived. The bus was almost empty, as he had been let out just before the rush hour really started. He sat upstairs at the front of the bus and was looking down rather enviously at the people zooming past in their cars when suddenly he received a painful blow on the back of his head. He jumped up and twisted round to confront the mad-woman who had delivered the blow. It was indeed a madwoman who had hit him, but Dempsey realized at once that he was in no danger. The madwoman was sixty, bearded and very drunk. She had accident-ally hit Dempsey on the back of the head while trying to swing one of her plastic bags over onto the seat next to her. The blow had been so painful because the bag contained the old woman's stone collection. As soon as Dempsey jumped up she began apologizing profusely. Dempsey insisted that he was alright and told her that he was just a bit on edge that day but she wouldn't rest until he had accepted one of her stones. Eventually Dempsey took one and thanked her for it. He was relieved to get off.

Before returning to his apartment, Dempsey stopped off at his corner shop (he referred to it as the drugstore) to buy a few things. He picked up a basket by the door and wished that he'd made a list. He remembered toothpaste. He went over to where the toothpaste was and picked up the nearest tube. On the box a man with a set of teeth that he would probably have been able to catch rabbits with, bub-bled the praises of some new waste product of the pharmaceutical industry. Dempsey was reminded of something. It was the teeth again. He dropped the box into his basket as if it was radioactivity that had made the rabbit-hunter's teeth glow in such a way. He remembered that he had to do his washing that evening. He would need washing powder. He marvelled at his powers of extrapolation. He picked up a square box emblazoned with a picture of a forty year old woman worryingly over-excited by the state of her husband's boxer-shorts. Dempsey was reminded of Mrs Barret. He dumped her next to the image of her husband in the wire basket and moved off towards the check-out counter. But, looking down at the contents of the basket, he felt that they really weren't going to make for a very exciting evening, so he added a few beers and topped it up with a couple of TV dinners out of the freezer. It felt just like home, but cost more.

Nearing the top of the stairs up to his landing, Dempsey heard the telephone ringing inside his apartment. He rushed to the door, dumped down his groceries and unlocked it. Inside, he turned on the light and raced down the hall to his bedroom. He dived across the bed and snatched the telphone off the bedside table. Touchdown he thought to himself.

'Yo Dempsey,' he said to whoever was on the other end of the telephone. But there was no one on the other end of the line; all that he could hear was the dialling tone. He took the telephone away from his ear and looked at it accusingly. He hadn't even heard a click, so he told himself that the caller was probably in the process of putting the phone down just as he was picking it up. Perhaps his phone was broken. Perhaps the person who had been trying to call him had a broken phone. There were hundreds of explanations that he could think of but there was also one that he didn't want to think of.

He traipsed back into the hall to retrieve his groceries. He opened the door casually and bent down and round the door frame to pick them up. Suddenly he noticed out of the corner of his eye that there was a small figure dressed in black standing and watching him intently, not ten feet along the landing. He started back, spilling the groceries and was about to slam the door when he recognized the figure. It was Foley, the building's janitor. He was just standing there in his black boiler suit staring at Dempsey like a bemused parrot. Dempsey recovered his composure. Foley had a theory that all Americans were mad and Dempsey could see that he had just added more fuel to the fire. He did feel a little foolish because it was difficult to imagine a less frightening figure than Foley. He was very short, only about five-foot-two, though he always claimed that he used to be five-foot-eight and had shrunk. He was also very old, about seventy-five, though he always claimed that he was only sixty. His most noticeable feature was his eyes. They were large and watery and exuded a kind of thoughtful stupidity. They reminded Dempsey of something which he couldn't quite put his finger on. Suddenly he put his finger on it — it was George, the Barret's basset hound. He took his finger off it.

'What's her name then?' asked Foley before Dempsey had had a chance to dispel the image from his mind.

'What?'

A strange expression came over Foley's face and he made a sudden movement. Dempsey started back again. But there was no need to worry. Foley hadn't drawn a gun, in fact he'd produced a bunch of flowers from behind his back. He stood there like a magician, though Dempsey still couldn't help thinking of him as a performing dog. But when Dempsey looked more closely at the flowers he realized that they were not supposed to be a joke. They were white Arum lilies. Dempsey didn't go in much for the language of flowers but he knew what these ones meant. He couldn't have got the message more clearly if he'd been sent a wreath.

'Where did these come from?' he asked Foley sharply. Foley looked rather crestfallen. He'd expected Dempsey to be pleased with his little surprise.

'They were delivered about half an hour ago.'

'By who?'

'The boy from the florists.' Foley looked down at the flowers and stroked the fat flesh mournfully. 'I haven't seen such lilies since Mrs Foley died.' He tried to think of his wife but all that he could remember of her was her funeral. He dragged himself back to the present.

'Don't want any carpets cleaned do ya?' he asked.

'What? Oh ... er, no thanks,' replied Dempsey. He'd just noticed that there was a card tucked in amongst the lilies.

He carried them inside, holding them as far away from his body as possible, as if they were contagious. He was just about to shut the door when Foley's head reappeared through the gap, startling him for the third time. 'Don't forget your groceries,' it said and then disappeared again.

Dempsey placed the lilies on the sideboard in the kitchen and then went back for the groceries. He plonked them down next to the lilies and plucked out the note. He opened up the envelope. Inside was a card with a bright red lipstick kiss on. He turned it over. There was no writing. Dempsey didn't know much about different lipstick shades or about the science of lip prints but he didn't need to know these things to tell that this was either the work of someone who watched too much television or someone who was mentally unhinged, or both. He didn't believe that the two were entirely unconnected.

Dempsey made a mental note to phone up the florists in the morning. He doubted that it would lead to anything, but perhaps, if the woman was sufficiently flipped, then she may have left her name, address and where she could be contacted in case of emergency. Dempsey crumpled up the card with the lip print on and hurled it at the waste-paper basket. It was a good shot but it bounced out. It was one of those days.

He strolled back into the living room and picked up an old sweat-shirt and towel that he'd left lying on his gym equipment. He decided that he'd try and lose himself in domestic chores. He had to do some washing and cleaning anyhow, so he wasn't really allowing her to alter the pattern of his life. He wasn't giving her that satisfaction and at least he might be able to forget her voice for a moment. He had listened to it too often and it was now replaying itself over and over again in his mind. He went into his bedroom and bundled all his dirty clothes into the suitcase on the floor. Then he took off the shirt that he was wearing and bunged that in as well. A sudden wave of nausea came over him as he picked up the shirt that he had changed out of earlier that day and saw the clotted blood. A man standing next to him in the bus queue had had his brains blown out and here he was setting off to do his washing. He stopped himself thinking along those lines. He knew it wasn't good for him. He thought of sex instead and gradually he began to feel better. He put on his last clean shirt, jammed the suitcase closed, grabbed his book and his washing money and left.

The launderette was situated deep in the bowels of Dempsey's mansion block. Normally it was a warm foetal place. It gave Dempsey a chance to meet the other residents on equal terms. Everybody could see everybody else's dirty laundry. Tonight the launderette was chill and empty. Dempsey loaded his machine, started it off and sat down to read his book.

Fifteen minutes later Dempsey looked at the front of his book in order to find out what he'd been reading. It was Edgar Allen Poe. He wondered why he was reading Edgar Allen Poe. He certainly wasn't enjoying the experience. Edgar Allen Poe was an American, sure, but Dempsey wasn't so nationalistic as to read only books written by Americans, and no way did he feel he had any duty to plough his way through the whole of American literature. The reason for him reading Edgar Allen Poe returned to him in a flash. It was because Makepeace kept quoting it at him and made him feel a couple of bricks short of a full load when he told her that he'd never read any. Well he'd read some of it now and now he knew why he hadn't got around to reading any of it before. It wasn't worth getting around to. *The Fall of the House of Usher* was ... His thoughts were interrupted by something. At first he couldn't work out what. Then he realized. It was getting darker. He looked up at the single bare bulb. It seemed to be dimming as he watched. He looked down at his book again. Yes, it was definitely dimming. If the bulb was about to go then that meant that he'd have to grope around in the dark to retrieve his washing. He stared at it and willed the element to hang on for a few more minutes. It

64

suddenly flashed back to full strength and Dempsey breathed a sigh of relief.

The relief was short lived. Dempsey was startled by an unexpected and deafening bang. Well it wasn't actually deafening, but its unexpected nature and the fact that Dempsey had been put on edge by the flickering of the lightbulb made it sound deafening to him. Dempsey leapt to his feet and prepared to grapple with his assailant or at least try to dodge the next bullet. He suddenly became glad that the launderette was empty. The noise that he'd found so frightening was only his washing-machine cutting out and the door lock releasing. He glanced down at Edgar Allen Poe accusingly. Now he understood how frightening television programmes could be a bad influence on young children.

He strolled over to his washing-machine and casually unloaded the clean, but still damp, clothes. He tried to relax his mind by first relaxing his body. Someone started up the lift. You could hear it in the launderette because the lift shaft started off down in the basement. Dempsey paid it no attention. He placed the basket containing his wet clothes into the tumble drier, twisted it through one hundred and eighty degrees and removed it, now empty of clothes. He found the economy of effort very satisfying.

The lift came to a noisy halt at the bottom of the shaft. Dempsey turned to see who got out. But the door remained shut and the lift silent. The lightbulb began to flicker again. Dempsey reached slowly for his gun but it wasn't there. He'd taken it off to change his shirt. He could have kicked himself but didn't as it would make too much noise. He tried to think about things objectively. The fact that the madwoman knew where he lived, as evidenced by the flowers, had made him rather jumpy. But he couldn't start getting trigger-happy every time a lift door didn't open. He remembered that, when he was a kid, whenever he saw a lift he used to rush into it, press all the buttons and then rush out again before the doors closed. He'd taken wicked satisfaction in the fact that everybody who got on the lift afterwards would have to stop at every floor. He told himself that it was kids having some harmless fun. All the same he suspected that he might be lying just to make himself feel better.

He skirted round the outside of the lift door until he was standing right in front of it. The lift light appeared to be broken. But down there in the basement the lift door, which was just an ordinary hinged one, was edged with perspex. It was dirty and scratched but in the darkness Dempsey thought that he could just make out. ... The bulb went with a faint metallic click, throwing the launderette into almost complete darkness. The only dim light came from the door that led to the bottom of the fire escape. Dempsey stood motionless trying to accustom his eyes to the gloom. The sound of his own breathing seemed deafening but he could hear no noise coming from the lift. He approached it stealthily on the balls of his feet, so as he could dive out of the firing line as quickly as possible. Still there was no sound or movement.

He decided to speak. 'Hello?' His voice echoed within the concrete walls, but there was no reply. 'Is anybody there?' Still nothing.

Dempsey moved closer and put his hand on the cold handle of the lift door. He took a silent breath and threw it open. A body leapt out at him. He jumped to one side and punched it as it flew past him. It was just a roll of carpet. He felt a wave of relief sweep over him, quickly followed by one of annoyance at letting his fears gain the upper hand over his reason.

'Hello,' came a voice down the lift shaft. It was Foley.

'Hello, Mr Foley,' shouted back Dempsey.

'Who's that?' enquired Foley.

'Dempsey.'

'Have you seen a carpet of mine Mr Dempsey?'

'Yeah,' said Dempsey, kicking it with his foot. 'I almost killed it.'

'What?'

'I said I almost. . . .' Dempsey decided that it wasn't worth it. 'Yeah it's down here Mr Foley. Press the button and I'll send it back up to you.'

'Thank you very much Mr Dempsey,' came back the reply.

Dempsey manhandled the heavy roll of carpet back into the lift and gave it another punch for good measure. But before he shut the door he shouted up the shaft again. 'Hey Mr Foley I'll swap your carpet for a lightbulb.'

Drying done, Dempsey climbed the stairs back up to his apartment. He swore. He could hear his telephone ringing again. He dumped his washing, opened the door, turned on the light, dashed down the hall and dived across the bed, as before. He reckoned that he must be improving. This time he heard the click as the person at the other end put the phone down.

He rolled over onto his back. Between him and the telephone this hadn't been a good day. In fact it hadn't been a good day for Americans as a whole. First him, then Edgar Allen Poe and now Alexander

Graham Bell. Dempsey wondered whether Alexander Graham Bell would ever have invented the telephone if he'd known the kind of things people would get up to with it.

But he decided that he couldn't go through life being afraid of the phone. He grabbed the main body of the telephone from his bedside table and placed it in front of him on the bed. He punched out a number. The telephone rang three times before it was answered.

'Hello.' It was Makepeace's voice.

'Harry?'

'Dempsey?'

Dempsey smiled. It was good to hear the sound of her voice. Though he wasn't sure he liked the way that she called him Dempsey and never Jim or James. But he wasn't ringing her to talk to her about that. 'Listen — you just try to call me?'

'No — must've been one of your other girls.'

Dempsey thought that she almost sounded jealous. 'Ah you're my only girl, you know that.' He paused for the sharp reply, but none was forthcoming, so he continued. 'Listen how about a movie tonight?'

'Er,' she hesitated and Dempsey reckoned that she was either thinking of a way of getting out of something else in order to go to the movies with him or a way of getting into something else in order not to go to the movies with him. 'I've got the decorators coming tomorrow. Um I'm busy moving everything, I'm sorry.'

'That's OK,' assured Dempsey, resigning himself to a night alone. 'I'll see you tomorrow.'

'Night.' She hung up.

Dempsey put his phone down as well. He was beginning to dislike the sound of the dialling tone. He wandered to his bedroom window and looked out. It had grown dark, but the sky was clear and the moon almost full. He looked at the windows of the mansion block opposite. Lots of people seemed to be staying in that night. Lots of people seemed to stay in every night. The blue light of their television sets flickered eerily through their front windows, it was as if they all had their own little moons there in their front rooms. He wondered whether Mrs Barret was watching television at that moment. A sudden feeling of depression welled up inside him. He decided that he wouldn't watch television that evening. He would tidy up his bathroom and read a book or something; not Edgar Allen Poe, though. He looked up and down the road again. Everyone leading their own separate lives. He couldn't work out whether that was a good or a bad thing.

But the life being lived in one of the windows opposite his wasn't as separate as he thought and that was definitely a bad thing, for him at least. Catherine Warren watched him standing at the window. She could have blown him away there and then. It was an easier shot than the one that she had attempted that morning. But fortunately for Dempsey she didn't feel in the mood. Dempsey walked away fom the window and she sat down. Her chair was positioned so as to give a good view of his window. Although he was unlikely to see her, there was a chance that he might of course, but Cathering Warren liked taking chances. She picked up an eight-by-ten black-and-white photograph of Dempsey that lay on the table beside her. She stuck a pin through his eyes and held the photograph up against the light. It shone through the pinholes. She resolved to try and shoot him through the eyes. It seemed rather poetic to her, a bit like a Greek myth or something.

Chapter
FOUR

Dempsey slept badly that night. He didn't dream of
Makepeace. His dreams were fast and confused,
peopled by men and women who yo-yoed furiously
between laughter and tears. Demspey was glad to
wake up. He didn't try to remember his dreams and
he didn't want them interpreted. If he was going mad,
he didn't want to know about it.

'Morning.' He hailed Spikings as heartily as possible, on bumping into him in the 'shop' car park.

'Sleep OK?' asked Spikings.

'Like a log, thanks.' Dempsey walked to where his
Mercedes was parked. It had been towed in that
morning for inspection. Dempsey had had to phone a
taxi. The SI10 mechanic had just opened the bonnet
to try and discover what had gone wrong with it.

'It might well be the distributor,' advised Dempsey
unhelpfully. The mechanic threw him a withering
look. Dempsey dodged it and continued with his

70

instructions. 'I wanna know if anything's been messed with — if anything's been done I wanna know about it. I'll call you in about an hour.'

'Sure, I should be able to find out something by then,' replied the mechanic, glad to be left to do his job in peace.

Dempsey made his way towards the building. Spikings was waiting for him by the door. He looked serious. Dempsey stopped in front of him, Spikings obviously had something on his mind.

'No man is an island. Poetry,' said Spikings in his normal direct and matter of fact manner.

Dempsey was taken aback. 'Poetry?' he repeated. He thought about it for a moment but couldn't spot the relevance. He shook his head. 'I don't follow.'

'Apropos of the girl's voice on the phone yesterday,' replied Spikings, as if elucidating the matter.

Dempsey looked even more puzzled. 'I'm sorry I still don't follow.'

Spikings set off towards his office at a brisk pace. Dempsey followed. Spikings continued. 'Well a single man. ....' Spikings was wrestling with something that he was not used to talking about. '... in London ...' He wrung his hands as if it would improve his eloquence. It didn't appear to. '... a long way from home. ...'

Dempsey was suddenly reminded of the time that his old man tried to tell him the facts of life. He'd known them already of course, in fact he'd made quite a bit of money by selling them to the other kids on his block, in two installments, but he'd let his father continue because he'd reckoned that it was probably good for him. He wasn't at all sure if what Spikings was trying to tell him was good for him, the poor man had gone almost puce in the face. But

Dempsey didn't interrupt him, chiefly because he didn't know what the hell he was trying to get at.

'... lots of pressure. ...' Spikings stumbled on. '... lots of temptations ... we're all human. ...'

'We are?' interrupted Dempsey, trying to lighten things up a bit.

Spikings could tell that he wasn't getting through. He disliked it when Dempsey was flippant, particularly when he was trying to be serious. He decided to try a different tack. 'We all react in different ways you know.'

'Do we?' responded Dempsey, still not over-amazed by Spikings' insights into human nature.

Spikings ignored him. 'With me it was fish,' he admitted.

'Fish?!' This time Dempsey really was amazed. He hoped that Spikings wasn't about to confess something awful to him.

'Trout. Had a two piece fibreglass rod. Whisky bait. Great way of working out your frustrations ... hang overs ... sifting through a problem.'

'I'll try it some time,' replied Dempsey warily. He wasn't at all sure why Spikings had chosen this moment to talk to him about fish but he thought it wisest to humour him.

'Umm — still a member ...' continued Spikings, '... a paid up member of the piscatorial society ... so er ...' Spikings was fishing for something more than fish. 'So if er ... there's anything you want to get off your chest ... feel free.'

At last Dempsey understood what Spikings was trying to get at. He thought that Dempsey was holding something back and was trying some kind of softly, softly approach to winkle it out of him. It was a project that was doomed from the start. Dempsey wasn't keeping anything back and, if he had been, then he knew better than anyone that Spiking was really a pumice stone underneath all that soft soap. Dempsey also objected to the fact that Spikings thought that he might have been lying to them. He wasn't above lying, of course, when lying was called for, but the fact was that this time he was telling the truth and he was indignant that they didn't believe him. He thought of telling Spikings how he felt about this, but Spikings was looking at him in such an avuncular way that he couldn't bring himself to do so. Instead he tried to pander to Spikings' obvious desire for some kind of confession.

'It's occurred to me,' he said thoughtfully, 'that this could be a contract out of New York.'

That idea had occurred to Spikings as well. 'No, no, no,' Spikings shook his head, 'I cabled New York about your little problem — nothing known at all.'

Dempsey felt relieved that there wasn't a New York hit man after him but also disappointed that they still had so little information to go on. Spikings watched these different emotions play across his features. Dempsey turned to him. 'Well if that's true then you can rest assured that if I can tie up that broad's voice to anyone I know ... or have known ... then you'll be the second person to know about it.'

Spikings looked pleased at receiving this confidence. But as Dempsey moved off, Spikings realized that what he'd just heard wasn't really what he'd wanted or expected to hear. He pulled Dempsey back by the arm. 'Who'll be the first then?'

'She will,' replied Dempsey menacingly and continued on up the corridor towards the central office.

Spikings stared up the corridor after him. He knew that it wasn't a good sign when coppers decided to deal with things privately. Even if they were things that infringed on their own private lives they should be dealt with through the proper channels. He hoped that Dempsey wasn't going to turn vigilante on him. He followed him into the central office and then entered his own office. A few minutes later he leant out of the door and yelled for Makepeace.

When she re-emerged from Spikings' office, Dempsey was busy tidying his desk again. 'Continuing with the mothering ploy then are you?' he asked without looking up.

She smiled. 'No we thought that we might try the paternal approach this time.'

'Spikings has already tried that one this morning.'

'And did you go for the slipper, or the ruler across the knuckles?'

'Oh, he said that you were the one who was going to deal out the punishment.'

'Actually I'm more in favour of the caring and sharing approach.' She emphasised sharing.

'You just won't take my word for it will you. Do you think that I'd be sitting here, fooling around with paperclips and elastic bands, if I had even the faintest idea of whose that voice was?' He scattered the recently tidied paperclips angrily across his desk.

'Hey calm down,' soothed Makepeace. 'I'm your partner. I believe that you're telling the truth. It's Spikings who's not too sure. All I'm worried about is that you'll do something stupid or hasty in your eagerness to catch this woman.'

He looked into her eyes. She really did seem concerned for his safety. He smiled at her. He was concerned about her safety as well. Just then the phone rang. He snatched it up and Makepeace went to collect the morning mail.

'Yo — Dempsey,' he said cheerfully, forgetting about his experiences with this phone the previous night. It was the SI10 mechanic. He embarked on a long and complicated explanation. 'Hey come on — cut the flibbits,' interrupted Dempsey. He hated the way that specialists in certain fields always tried to blind you with science or baffle you with strange terms. 'One question. Was the engine tampered with or not?' Dempsey raised his eyes to the ceiling in despair. 'Could have been ...' he mimicked the tone of the mechanic, '... maybe. Hey thanks a lot, you know — you're a real wonder.' The mechanic became indignant. Dempsey tried to soothe him. 'All right ... all right. Did you do anything with the clock?' The mechanic told him that for that kind of work he should go elsewhere, though where he suggested didn't sound like the kind of place that would have many garages. Dempsey held the phone away from his ear until the bellowing was replaced by the dialling tone. He knew that one day either the British or their dialling tone would drive him mad. He put the phone back on the hook. Makepeace entered with the mail. She flicked through the pile and handed one to Dempsey.

'Gosh, he knows somebody that writes,' she said sarcastically. He riposted with a grimace. She wasn't far off though. He wasn't sure that he did know many people who wrote letters anymore. Especially people who would write to him at SI10.

Makepeace watched as he opened it. As soon as he'd pulled the letter from its envelope his face seemed to pale and his eyes widened. He shoved it straight into his pocket without reading it. He noticed that Makepeace had been watching him.

'My aunt. She's just got into town. Never been

75

here before. Wants me to have dinner with her,' he explained unconvincingly.

Makepeace had come across Dempsey's aunts before. Everytime a girl phoned him up it normally turned out to be one of his aunts. The younger ones were his cousins. Dempsey seemed to have a big family. Dempsey knew that Makepeace doubted the size of his family and that was why he'd used that excuse then. But Makepeace wasn't so easily fooled by the double bluff. She knew that it wasn't from his aunt but she also sensed that the letter wasn't from a girlfriend either or at least, if it was from a girlfriend, then it was from a girlfriend that Dempsey was pretty scared of.

Dempsey tapped the clock in his Mercedes. Perhaps the man had felt guilty and mended it after all. He hadn't. That was part of the trouble with Britain today, reflected Dempsey, every job was tied down by hundreds of rules, regulations and union directives. It avoided exploitation, admittedly, but it did nothing for employee/employer relations. Dempsey tapped the clock again, this time a little harder. He thought that he might turn back and attempt a reasoned and reasonable discussion with the mechanic who'd refused to fix it. Maybe he'd go back and thump him instead.

He turned left and came to a halt in front of St Hilda's secondary school for girls. He felt that he should have guessed it. It was deserted and scheduled for demolition. He pulled the crumpled letter out of his pocket. The bright red lips pouted out at him. 'St Hilda's secondary school for girls. 11:30 a.m.' That was all it said. He looked down at the car clock and then at his watch. It was 11.29 a.m. He pulled his Magnum from his holster, checked the magazine once again and slid it back beneath his arm. He got out of the car, screwed up the letter and threw it into a litter bin attached to a nearby lamppost. The letter fell to the ground. It was a run down area. Even the litter bins had been vandalized. The bottom had fallen out of everything. Dempsey contemplated picking the letter up. He wondered whether he should have kept the card as well, the one with the other lip print on, in order to compare the two set of prints. But he rejected the idea. He reckoned that he would go mad himself if he found out that there were two mad women after his blood, each with the same line in cheap, but scary, theatrics. He kicked the screwed up piece of paper into the gutter and pushed open the school gates. They creaked loudly. Dempsey was reminded of Edgar Allen Poe. Though on second thoughts it was more like Alan Bleasedale, without the jokes.

The gates swung closed behind him. Dempsey stood motionless at the end of the playground and surveyed the scene. In front of him stood a large four-storey Victorian Gothic building. The maroon brick should really have been draped in ivy. Instead it was covered in graffiti. All the windows were broken and much of the roof was missing. If the building hadn't been in the heart of the run-down inner city but in the rolling Suffolk countryside it might have looked haunted. As it was it was still frightening but for lots of other and more real reasons. To either side of this building, and making up two other sides of the square of the playground, stood two nineteen-sixties pre-fabricated classroom blocks. They were even more run-down than the main building. They had both been gutted by fire and were now no more than shells.

So it was in the centre building that Dempsey had his rendezvous. He walked slowly towards the central door. He began to wish that he hadn't come or that at least he'd not been so stupid as to come without back up. He glanced up at all the high buildings from which someone could get a clear shot of him. He saw no one but then he didn't know where to look and she did. He felt that he was worse off than Gary Cooper in *High Noon.* With Cooper it had been three against one admittedly, but in his case there hadn't been any snipers with high powered rifles and telescopic sights either. The walk across the playground seemed a very long one and one his legs weren't too keen on making. Still, for some perverse reason he felt fairly safe out there in the open with the nearest cover at least twenty yards away. He didn't really understand the workings of his adversary's mad mind, but it seemed to him to work on a kind of reverse logic. The first shot, the one that had killed Theodore Barret, had been totally out of the blue. So, now he'd been notified, he didn't reckon that he'd be shot at. He didn't really belive it himself but he thought that it would help him make it to the door.

He made it, just as Gary Cooper had done before him. He collapsed against the wall by the door and took a few deep breaths to steady himself and then reached for his gun. He was sweating profusely. He clasped the Magnum in both hands and leant back against the wall again, pressing the cool barrel against his nose and trying to prepare himself for whatever was going to come next. From a distance it looked as if he was praying. In a way he was.

He took one last lungful, pushed himself off from the wall and kicked open one half of the double door, darting behind the other half for cover. The door slammed against its door stop and swung swifly shut again. Nothing stirred inside. Dempsey pushed the door open again but this time more gently. Again it hit against the door stop and swung back, but this time as the gap between the doors narrowed, Dempsey slipped inside the building.

He crouched down on his haunches swinging his gun from side to side blindly in front of him, trying to fend off the invisible enemy. Slowly his eyes became accustomed to the darkness and the shadows skulked away from even the darkest recesses of the hall. It was empty and derelict and there was no sign of recent human presence apart from the stink of piss. Dempsey stood up carefully and prepared to search the ground-floor rooms. Suddenly he stopped dead in his tracks. He'd heard the front gates creaking open. It might have been the wind but he reckoned that he would feel pretty stupid if he was blown away and it wasn't by the wind. He made his way back towards the front door, taking care to avoid being seen through the windows. As he did so he became aware of another, far more sinister sound. It was so quiet that, at first, it had only entered his sub-conscious, playing as background music to his thoughts, but as he approached the front door again the sound grew louder and his conscious mind became aware of it. He shuddered. Upstairs, someone was playing a piano. He knew that it was her. An organ might have gone better with the lilies but a piano was obviously more portable and would serve. She was pulling out all the cliches, but so was he; he decided to investigate.

The main staircase was large and open and swept up both sides of the entrance hall. It was the kind of staircase that Cinderella might leave her footwear on. Well it was the same shape anyhow. Dempsey began to climb it. He took the left-hand side and kept his eyes firmly fixed on the balcony of the floor above from which the sound seemed to emanate. He slid his back along the wall to give himself a better angle of view. Any moment he expected a mad woman shrieking wildly, dressed in rags and with long black hair to come rushing onto the balcony and take pot shots at him. She didn't. Dempsey made it safely to the top of the stairs and as he did so the music stopped.

He stared along the corridor from which the sound had come. It wasn't inviting. The smell of urine that he had noticed downstairs was even stronger up here. But up here there was also something else mingled with it. Dempsey tried to place the smell. It was glue. People had been indulging in solvent abuse up there. Dempsey laughed inwardly at the phrase coined by people who thought that Evo-stick was only used for mending croquet mallets.

Dempsey looked around him, waiting for the piano to start up again. The floor was littered with crisp packets. They all seemed to be roast chicken flavour. Dempsey wondered whether roast chicken went best with glue. He tried to wonder some more, but knew that he was just procrastinating. He was relatively safe up there on the balcony. If she came for him there, he knew that he'd be in command. He didn't want to have to go along that corridor and poke his head round every door, each time expecting to get it blown off.

There were five doors off the corridor, two either side and one at the end. Dempsey decided to start with the first door on the left. He picked his way carefully through the rubbish, taking care not to step on any of the crisp packets and give away his position. As he approached the door he could see that it already had a large hole in the top panel. He picked up the piece of wood that seemed to have been kicked from the door and was now lying on the corridor floor. He waved the piece of wood in front of the hole, all the time expecting it to be blown out of his hand. It wasn't. The room remained silent, so Dempsey waved his hand quickly in front of the hole. He thought that she might have been waiting for the sight of flesh, but there was still no reaction. He peered through the hole, first with one eye and then with both. He felt rather foolish. He found himself peering into a broom cupboard only a foot wider than the door itself. The small window at the back of the cupboard had been kicked in as well. The light from it reflected off something on the floor. Dempsey looked closer. The floor was covered in flattened and charred bits of silver paper. This was the room where they 'chased the dragon.' It was a squalid place for a squalid habit with a misleadingly romantic name.

Dempsey looked around at the other four doors. He wondered what lay in wait for him behind them. As he progressed further into the building things seemed to be getting worse and worse, he dreaded to think what horrors lurked in the room at the end of the corridor. He moved towards the next door, the first on the right. He rather hoped that all the doors opened onto empty broom cupboards, but as he grabbed hold of the handle of this next one he heard a faint sound from inside. He darted behind the safety of the wall. He'd seen people blown away through doors in his time. He listened again, but heard nothing. He began to wonder whether it had been his imagination, but then the sound came again, very faint, but definitely real. It sounded to him like someone was stalking around inside. He took his courage, and his magnum, in both hands and threw open the door. As he did so some thirty pigeons took to the air. Most flew out of a vast hole in the wall through which they'd entered, but a few confused and foolish pigeons flew out of the very door that had frightened them into flight. They flew within a foot of Dempsey's face. He felt the downdraft created by their wings as they passed and they very nearly felt the sting of hot lead. Dempsey prevented himself from pulling the trigger just in time. The adrenalin in his system had made his reactions hyperquick, but fortunately for the pigeons he was thinking even quicker.

Dempsey entered the room just vacated by the pigeons. He knew that there was no one in there because they would have scared the pigeons off. There was nothing special about the room. It was an old classroom that had become a lavatory for birds. Still, Dempsey felt safe in there. He could cross that room off his list but the odds on the other three rooms were shortening. A pigeon returned to perch on the edge of the hole in the wall and stare questioningly at the absurdity of Dempsey's antics. Dempsey decided that he hated pigeons; pigeons and cats. They always had one of the two in horror movies and they always caused unnecessary anxiety. Two more pigeons joined the first. Dempsey decided to press on. He wasn't going to turn chicken on account of a few pigeons. He re-entered the corridor and made his way towards the third door.

He'd gone about three yards when he froze suddenly in his tracks. There was someone in the hall downstairs. All the hairs on his body felt as if they were standing on end and his heart began to race. He told himself that it was just the pigeons, but his sense of logic told him that it couldn't possibly be; the sound was being made by something heavy, something as heavy as a man. He began to turn slowly, in order to make his way back along the corridor. He didn't want to believe that there were two people. He told himself that the acoustics of the building could be misleading; it was in such bad disrepair that floors might be missing and the piano could in fact have been played downstairs. Suddenly and terrifyingly all his self-delusions were shown to be just that. The piano started up again. It was definitely coming from the room at the end of the corridor. Dempsey didn't know which way to turn. He was trapped. His heart leapt up into his mouth and a clammy covering of sweat sprang up all over his body. He tried to swallow but his saliva had dried up and he didn't want to swallow his heart. He tossed a coin in his mind. He'd shoot the piano player first.

He turned back to the door at the end of the corridor and picked his way towards it. Occasionally he twisted his head round quickly and violently to see if the other person had reached the top of the stairs. It was like some macabre game of grandmother's foot-steps. He reached the door and still there was no sign of the person he had heard downstairs. By now his body was pouring sweat. It dripped from his upper lip into his mouth. He knew what they meant by the taste of fear. His gun had become slippery in his hand. He transferred it to his other hand and dried his gun hand on his jacket. He transferred the gun back and gripped it tightly; now wasn't the time to drop it. The piano player continued unabated. She, or per-haps he, was rather good. Dempsey hoped that he wouldn't have to blow their brains out. He took hold of the door handle just as he had done with the pre-vious room. This time, however, he knew that on the other side there was something more dangerous than pigeons. The music stopped.

He flung the door open. The wall on the other side of the door exploded. The piano player was also a soloist on the sawn-off shotgun. Dempsey hurled himself across the doorway before she had a chance to empty the other barrel of the gun into the wall his side of the door. As he flew past the entrance he pumped two shots in roughly the direction of his would-be assassin. He couldn't make out anything amongst the dust and smoke. He heard no movement inside. He lay on his stomach, gun at the ready, beneath the hole made by the first blast and looked up at it. His mind was racing at the same pace as his heart. Whoever had chosen to shoot through that side of the door didn't know much about police methods; no one stood that side of the door as it made it much more difficult to push the door open quickly and safely. The smoke and dust pouring through the shotgun hole made the light seem solid. Something struck Dempsey as being peculiar about the hole. Of course, it wasn't round it was oval; that meant that both barrels of a shotgun had been fired off simultaneously, not just one. He knew that double-barrelled pump-action shotguns didn't exist and therefore he concluded that whoever was inside was now reloading.

Dempsey leapt to his feet and dived through the open doorway, rolling as he landed, just in case the firer of the shotgun was a quicker reloader than he hoped. He saw the shotgun barrel glint in the sunlight that streamed through the shattered windows and his finger tightened on the trigger. But he didn't fire. There was no one to fire at. The shotgun was just a booby trap. Dempsey lowered his gun and began to breathe again. The gun had been strapped to an old blackboard easel and connected to the door by a system of strings and pulleys. Simple but fortunately not effective.

Dempsey looked across to the hole blown in the

wall. The feeling of cold returned. For on the wall someone had painted a white chalk outline of a man. Dempsey could guess who it was supposed to be. The man had had his chest and stomach blown away. So it hadn't been just a miscalculation on behalf of the killer. She was playing with him. She knew how policemen worked right enough. Dempsey ran his hand around the inside of the hole wondering what it would have felt like if it had been him rather than this, his shadow. He reckoned that it would have been quick but messy. He drew back from the hole suddenly. He wondered if the madwoman was working some kind of voodoo on him, destroying his images and, by destroying them, gradually destroying him. He resolved there and then not to play into her hands by going it alone again. Then he had another thought. If he had brought Makepeace along on this one then she would have been standing the other side of the door. He looked at the silhouette again. It could have been anyone, even her. He was reminded of Theodore Barret dancing on the pavement.

He slid his gun back into his holster, glad that the man on the wall hadn't been provided with a partner on the floor. But just as he withdrew his hand, to his complete horror the piano started up again. He'd totally forgotten about the piano. He hadn't seen it when he'd rolled into the room as he'd been looking for another, more deadly instrument. For a fraction of a second he froze. Then in one movement, he turned, fell and pumped four bullets into the piano player. He was getting jumpy. The piano player turned out to be a cassette player attached to some kind of time clock. He walked over to what remained of it and rolled over its electrical entrails with his shoe. He wondered whether the woman's purpose was not to kill him but to drive him mad as well. Then they could get married and live madly ever after.

It was then that he heard the footsteps running up the corridor towards him. He remembered the second person, or rather the only person, the one whom he had heard in the hall downstairs. He recognized the footsteps as a woman's. He levelled his gun at the doorway. He calculated that she'd take a few fractions of a second to locate where he was standing in the room and if she had a gun another few fractions of a second to point it at him. He on the other hand knew exactly where she was going to appear. In other words he would be able to blow her away before she blew him away. The footsteps were nearly on him. He felt in control for the first time since he entered the school playground, his gun felt comfortable in his hands. The footsteps reached the door. The woman didn't stop, she dived through it about a foot from the ground, rolled across the floor and landed swiftly back on her feet again, her gun levelled at Dempsey's forehead. Dempsey was taken a bit by surprise by her entrance. He panned his gun across, tracking her and gradually tightened his finger on the trigger. They ended up face to face and gunpoint to gunpoint. Neither of them fired.

Makepeace was the first to lower her gun. She placed her hands on her hips and looked at Dempsey as if he'd just spilt coffee on her carpet, rather than nearly blown her head off. Dempsey lowered his gun slowly. He looked less relaxed. 'What are you doing here?' he asked, his vocal chords tight and this throat dry.

'Well where would the Lone Ranger be without Tonto?' replied Makepeace flippantly. She obviously didn't realize how close Dempsey had come to pulling the trigger.

'The Lone Ranger almost blew Tonto away, what would have happened to the TV series then?' He slid his gun back into the holster and took in a deep breath to try and steady himself.

Makepeace strolled casually around the room. She pulled the string that worked the booby trap and the shotgun hammer clicked. She tilted her head admiringly and looked across at the hole in the wall. She ran her fingers around the inside of it just as Dempsey had done previously. 'I see your girlfriend is a bit of an artist as well,' she remarked. She stood back from the silhouette in order to admire it. 'Not a bad likeness.'

'I don't think that my sternum is quite so depressed. Come on let's get out of here, this place gives me the creeps.'

Makepeace continued her inspection. She knew that it was annoying Dempsey but she felt that it served him right for running off on his own pretending he was Clint Eastwood. She examined what remained of the cassette player and bent down to read the label on the disembowelled cassette. 'Classical music, eh? She should have known that you weren't a great fan of classical music. Now if it had been Bruce Springsteen then that would have been a different matter completely. There would have been no need for this senseless waste of electrical equipment.' She looked up at Dempsey and grinned at him exaggeratedly. Dempsey stared back coldly. He knew why she was doing this to him. He deserved it but that didn't mean he was enjoying it.

'Look Harry, I'm sorry alright. I know that I should have told you about this one but I figured that it was kinda personal. You know what I mean.'

Makepeace was glad that he'd apologized but an

apology wasn't enough for putting them both in a position where they might have killed each other.

'No I don't know what you mean,' she snapped back. 'This isn't the Wild West you know, Dempsey. Personal vendettas went out with the Old Testament. Every crime is personal for someone and it's our job to be impersonal. Besides you obviously needed me. If that had been her diving through the door instead of me then you could well be dead. And then what would it matter how bloody personal it was?'

'Ah, but she couldn't possibly be as fast as you.' Dempsey tried to appease her with flattery but she would have none of it. She was angry.

'Don't give me that.' She stared at him coldly.

'OK, OK, I said that I was sorry. Next time I get an invitation to a party you can come as well. I promise. Now please can we get out of here. This place has bad memories for me.'

Makepeace seemed to accept his apology this time and relented. 'OK. But you better not do anything like this ever again.'

They made their way back along the corridor and down the stairs. The playground, which had seemed so sinister previously, was now just a playground again. Even the sun seemed brighter than when Dempsey had first entered the building. Perhaps it was just because it was higher in the sky. He glanced down at his watch. It was high noon. Dempsey smiled. He tried to engage Makepeace in conversation. He congratulated her on tailing him so well and on her entrance into the room, but she was still in no mood for flattery.

On exiting from the gates, they both stopped. There was something tucked underneath the windscreen-wiper of Dempsey's car and it wasn't a parking ticket. They both moved closer to find out what it was. It was an eight-by-ten black-and-white photograph of Dempsey. His eyes had been pierced with a pin and his mouth was smothered in a bright red lipstick kiss. They stared at it for a moment. There had been someone else in the building after all. The thought induced a sick feeling in both their stomachs.

Makepeace removed the photograph, taking care not to get her fingerprints on it, and looked at it more closely. 'Going to love you to death isn't she?'

Dempsey tried to muster a smile but couldn't manage it. He hoped that she wouldn't succeed.

Chapter
FIVE

The boys from forensics were on the scene as
promptly as ever, though Dempsey and Makepeace
could tell that they were a little disappointed not to
find a dead body they could paw over. They were also
a trifle disgruntled that the murder weapon, or more
accurately the weapon used in the attempted murder,
was still at the scene of the crime. They would have
preferred to try and deduce the make of shotgun and
type of cartridge from the shape of the blast hole and
the nature of the shotgun pellets. As it was, all they
had to do was to read the name engraved on the butt
of the gun and eject the cartridges. They did, however, admire the elegant simplicity of the booby trap
device, just as Dempsey and Makepeace had done
before them, but again there was still a feeling that
they might have preferred something radio-
controlled. They took the gun back to the laboratory
with them, even though they knew its make as they

hoped they might be able to find traces of hair or skin or, if they were really lucky, perhaps even blood on it. They found none of these things and nor did they find any fingerprints in the room, on the gun or on the photograph. They did think, however, that there was a slim chance that they might be able to trace the photograph, but it would take a bit of time. Dempsey told them to contact him at home if they came up with anything. Then, much to her surprise, he invited Makepeace to come back to his place for a cup of coffee. She began to wonder if she hadn't perhaps been too harsh with him earlier. She had only been to his flat once before and that had been a fleeting visit to pick up some stuff. He'd invited her round a few times before but she had always had other things on. She accepted his invitation gladly now though. She was curious to find out what his apartment looked like.

In fact the apartment wasn't quite as intriguing as she'd imagined. It was really quite inoffensive. She hadn't known what to expect, as her knowledge of the inside of American homes was derived entirely from films and television programmes. She knew that it wouldn't be like J.R.'s drawing-room or Rhoda's apartment, but her expectations had suggested something along the lines of Frank Cannon's bachelor pad. But, as it was, Dempsey's apartment was bright, clean and even verged on the sophisticated, although she would never have dreamed of telling him that. It wasn't her kind of apartment, though. The white walls looked slick but they didn't really feel very homely to her. Also there was a noticeable absence of personal effects, not the kind of things that you find in people's pockets when they are shot down at bus stops, but the bits of bric-à-brac that one tends to collect over the years, each with its own special memories. Makepeace was reminded of the Barrets' house. Dempsey's apartment was a real contrast. His only piece of bric-à-brac seemed to be a mounted baseball bat on the mantlepiece. It was also the only thing that revealed an American lived there.

She strolled through into the bedroom where Dempsey was changing his shirt. Blood yesterday and sweat today, Dempsey wondered what it would be tomorrow. He was glad that he'd tidied up his house before Makepeace had got to see it. Makepeace looked round the bedroom, trying to avoid looking at Dempsey's body. The bedroom was even emptier of personal effects than the other rooms. There weren't even any pictures on the wall. 'Bit Spartan isn't it?' she remarked. She looked across at the suitcase that lay on the floor, open but still with most of his washing in. 'Looks as if you're just passing through.'

Dempsey followed her gaze. He continued to do up his buttons. 'Yeah well hopefully I am. You ever read F. Scott Fitzgerald?'

Makepeace smiled at the question, it was normally her role to ask the literary questions. 'Yes,' she replied haughtily, as if Dempsey had just accused her of not eating with a knife and fork.

'Well Zelda Fitzgerald,' he continued, 'she used to say that she was never happy in a room that didn't have an open suitcase in it.'

'She went nutty — it says something about you,' she said smugly. She beamed broadly in his direction, pleased at her remark, and sauntered back along the hall towards the living-room again.

Dempsey watched her leave. At one stage he *had* thought that he was going nutty but it was good having her with him to keep his feet on the ground.

He smiled at his own literary pretensions. He only knew that Zelda Fitzgerald liked to have an open suitcase in her room because he'd seen a television documentary about her. He'd tried to beat Makepeace at her own game but he'd got his fingers burnt and it served him right. Still, it was a pleasanter sensation than the sweating palms he'd experienced earlier that day in the school.

'I didn't realize you had all this equipment.' Makepeace's voice interrupted his thoughts. Her voice came from the living-room but he wasn't sure what she meant by equipment. He grabbed his jacket and went to find out.

As he entered he saw Makepeace running her painted finger nails along the leather surface of the sit-up bench of his mini-gym. The gesture suddenly seemed very sensuous to him, though she was probably only checking for dust. Seeing Dempsey, Makepeace jerked her hand away just as if she'd been caught with her fingers in the cake mix.

'Do you mean I don't look as if I work out or I don't look as if I need to work out?' asked Dempsey with a grin. It was his turn to saunter. He sauntered into the kitchen and turned on the kettle. 'Coffee?'

'Yes, please,' accepted Makepeace from the living-room. She was glad to have the subject of conversation changed. She examined Dempsey's gym equipment more closely. She hadn't really noticed it when she'd first entered the room, even though it took up quite a large space. There were three separate pieces of equipment. Two that seemed to involve a system of weights and pullies and one which looked just like a bench with various extra bits to hook ones arms or legs or whatever around. It wasn't obvious what the exercises one could do on it were. There was something very attractive about all three of them to Makepeace. The combination of the leather and the metal cables and the matt-black blocks of weights made them look very slick and elegant, they were almost works of art in their own right. There was also something very sexual about them, but Makepeace didn't linger on that thought. She went to watch Dempsey making the coffee in the kitchen. It seemed to be rather an absurd task for a man who could also spend his evenings bench pressing two hundred-pound weights.

The kitchen was a typical bachelor kitchen; there was very little food, but numerous electrical devices. There *was* a kind of breakfast bar but it was more *Habitat* than *Frank Cannon*. Makepeace spotted the lilies, still in their wrapping paper, lying on the draining-board. 'Going to a funeral?' she asked flippantly, indicating the flowers to Dempsey.

'Could be my own.' He felt that he could afford a little B-movie melodrama in the safety of his own home. An Englishman's home is his castle and all that. Though Dempsey was an American, of course.

'Are they from . . .'

'What d'you think?' interrupted Dempsey.

'Traceable?' asked Makepeace, ignoring his condescending tone of voice.

'Ordered by phone. Money by taxi.' Dempsey felt himself slipping into Spikings' intonations. It was because he didn't like her treating him like an amateur.

'Sugar?' he asked, trying to manoeuvre the topic of conversation away from police business. He knew that she didn't take sugar and he knew that it annoyed her when he asked her whether she did.

Makepeace knew that he knew that it annoyed her

but before the game could proceed any further the kitchen telephone began to ring. Dempsey picked it up. 'Yo — Dempsey.'

It was someone in a phonebox. They didn't put any money in. The phone bleeped for a few seconds and then the dialling tone took over. Perhaps someone had tried to use a broken phone Dempsey told himself, though he wasn't entirely convinced. He put the phone down.

'Broken telephone,' he explained to Makepeace. She wasn't entirely convinced either. It wasn't like Dempsey to get worked up over what might only have been a warped ten-pence bit. She guessed that he suspected it was a warped mind. She remembered their phone conversation the previous night. In retrospect she recalled that he'd also sounded unaccountably worked up then. Still, he had good reason to be a little on edge, there was a madwoman out to kill him and they seemed to be no nearer finding out who she was, let alone apprehending her.

Makepeace squeezed the soft white flesh of one of the lilies absent-mindedly. She realized what she was doing and let go of the flower as if it had become hot in her hand. The bloody things not only symbolized death they felt like death as well. Dempsey stared thoughtfully into his cup of coffee. Makepeace walked behind him and casually picked up a crisp from the bowl on the sideboard and popped it into her mouth. It was stale and soggy and tasted revolting. She swallowed it quickly, hoping that it wasn't salmonella flavour. 'Eaargh, your crisps aren't crisp.'

'My crisps are chips,' corrected Dempsey.

'You say potato and I say potato,' chanted Makepeace. Both of them found these American/English arguments rather boring but neither of them was prepared to give in.

'No I didn't,' said Dempsey, not giving in, but not wishing to continue the argument at that particular moment. 'I say sit down and stop prowling around my kitchen like a health inspector.'

Makepeace sat down next to him at the kitchen table and picked up her cup of coffee. Dempsey was still deep in his own thoughts. She decided that this might be the moment to try and help jog his memory. 'A woman in love, or who thinks she's in love. You know what they say — "Hell hath no fury . . ."'

'Yeah but I ain't scorned nobody,' interrupted Dempsey. She was beginning to get him angry. He couldn't understand why she wouldn't believe him. Then he remembered not telling her about his little trip back to school.

'You ain't scorned nobody, *knowingly*,' continued Makepeace, imitating Dempsey's accent very badly.

Dempsey looked across at her fiercely but she was determined not to be put off. Dempsey recognized this determination and in a way admired her for it. The only trouble was he really couldn't think of anybody he'd scorned. He was tempted to throw her a false name in order to get her off his back, but he ruled this out as pure cowardice. He racked his brain again but could think of no one. He'd known a few screwy dames in his time, ones who seemed to get upset over nothing, but none of them seemed screwy enough to want to dispose of him just because they'd caught him eyeing up some other dame, or because, in the heat of the moment, he'd confused them with some old flame. They might have wanted to slap him around the face a little, they might even have done so, but he couldn't see any of them taking pot shots at him with a high-powered rifle. He shook his head. He could think of no one.

Makepeace watched him as he thought, it looked a painful process. She recognized that he really could think of no one whom he had scorned and though, judging from the number of aunts and cousins he seemed to have got through, she still thought that there must be someone, she decided it would be best to try and change the topic of conversation. If Dempsey left the thinking to his subconscious then a name might just pop up later on, and without the need for all the strained expressions.

'What about the photo?' Makepeace asked, trying to sound as if she was keen to hear Dempsey's erudite opinion on the matter.

'What about the photo?' echoed Dempsey blankly.

'Well how did she get hold of it?'

'You tell me,' he demanded. He wasn't being very helpful. Makepeace glowered at him. Sometimes he could behave like a pig-headed little kid, she thought to herself, but she was determined not to let him rile her.

'She took it,' she suggested.

'Or had it taken.' Dempsey was doing his best to be obstructive and his best wasn't bad. He did realize the import of the question, however, and his answer was, in a way, relevant. If she'd taken the photograph herself then it was very unlikely that records would be able to trace it. If, however, she'd hired someone else to take it, a photographer or more likely a private eye, then the photograph might, indeed, be traceable. But the chances were small and the photograph was still the only real lead that they had. Dempsey found it a depressing prospect but being obstructive helped cheer him up a bit.

Makepeace also realized the importance of being

able to trace the photograph but she too was working towards something else with her questioning. 'It was taken without you realizing?' she asked, her manner unperturbed by Dempsey's unhelpfulness.

Dempsey switched from obstructiveness to outright aggression. 'Of course I didn't realize. It was taken with a telephoto lens. The photo had a greatly fore-shortened perspective, you could have seen that for yourself. It's easy to take someone's photo without them being aware of it. Jesus, we've done it often enough ourselves.' Dempsey despaired of her. He wondered whether she was just trying to make conversation or whether there was something else she was trying to get at.

Seeing his anger and confusion Makepeace tried to jog his memory just one more time.

'Jilted girlfriend ... ex-lover. ...'

Dempsey howled down her suggestions. 'No, no, no.' But Makepeace wasn't going to be put off just by the number of decibels that her partner could generate.

'You don't believe it because you don't *want* to believe it,' she shouted back accusingly.

Dempsey stood up angrily. He was too irate to reply immediately and so he walked away from the table in order to try and calm down a little. Makepeace used this breathing space to regain her own cool also. Having composed himself to some extent, Dempsey walked back to the table. 'I don't believe it because it's not true.' He spoke the words inches from her face.

She smiled back at him calmly almost smirkingly. These were their original roles, she cool and calculating, he hot-tempered and hot-headed. The only trouble was that at the moment he wasn't particularly enjoying his role, especially as he felt that she'd tricked him into becoming hot-tempered. He placed his knuckles on the table in front of her and leant on them like a gorilla. He tried to shake her out of her apparent complacency and get her to shout at him again. It was a side of her that he rarely saw.

'You'd like me to start reeling off names and addresses wouldn't you?' he asked. But by this time Makepeace was coolness personified once again.

'Of course not.' Her voice was calm and earnest, school mistresslike. 'I just think that it might help.'

Dempsey slumped back down into his seat. 'Well contrary to what you might believe, I was not the Romeo of the New York Police Department.' Their eyes met. He thought that he detected disappointment. 'Though I could tell you some stories that would curl your hair,' he added.

'I've always wanted curly hair.'

'Well stick your finger in a wall socket then 'cos you ain't getting it from me.'

This time it was Makepeace's turn to stand up in frustration. She wasn't going to be put off by Dempsey's evasiveness and unwillingness to face the facts. She'd force him to admit that it was someone he knew, and probably someone whom he'd had some kind of relationship with, if it was the last thing she did. She knew that he'd feel that it was a blow to his masculinity if he found out that a woman who he'd had a relationship with was trying to kill him but she also knew that he couldn't let his own machismo get in the way of him being a good detective. She clenched her jaw muscles and glared down at him. To anyone watching through the kitchen window it would have looked like the archetypal lovers' quarrel.

She spoke to him through gritted teeth, slowly and

deliberately. 'The solution, whatever it is, wherever it is — lies with you! It has to!'

She was determined to force Dempsy into making some kind of acknowledgement of his part in the matter but Dempsey was equally determined to deny it. They stared at each other fiercely. The phone began to ring. The ferocity of their staring match lessened. It's difficult to conduct a really fierce staring match when a phone is ringing. It makes the whole thing seem rather absurd. Makepeace was the first to give in.

'You're phone's ringing.'

Dempsey glanced across at it and grunted but made no movement.

'Aren't you going to answer it?' asked Makepeace. It was beginning to annoy her.

'Nope.'

'Why not?'

'Because there's nobody on it.'

Makepeace suspected that he was just being churlish but she could also see that he really was determined not to answer it. Eventually the ringing became so irritating that she decided that she'd answer it herself. She hoped that it was one of his 'aunts' or 'cousins' and that they would be maddened by hearing another woman's voice. Though hopefully not sufficiently maddened to contemplate murder. She strolled over to the phone, picked it up and spoke into it as sexily as possible. She watched Dempsey to see what his reactions were. He looked apprehensive.

'I told you so,' said Dempsey, trying hard to conceal his smugness but not doing a very good job.

Makepeace handed him the phone. 'It's for you.'

Dempsey looked, and felt, stupid. He accepted the phone meekly. He made a mental note not to be too

100

self-confident when there was even the slightest chance of him being wrong, because, if there was even the slightest chance, then it was one hundred per cent sure to go against him.

'Yo, Dempsey ... Yeah?' he started to sound enthusiastic. Makepeace moved closer to try and find out what was going on. '... Yeah? ... that's great I'm on my way.' He put the phone down and grinned contentedly at Makepeace. She knew that he wasn't going to tell her, she'd have to ask.

'What's great?'

'They've traced the photograph.'

It was good news. They had their first real lead. Dempsey rushed to the door. Makepeace followed him, but not with quite the same urgency. She still hadn't made Dempsey admit the possibility that the woman who was after him was one whom he'd probably been after in the past. Dempsey waited for her by the front door.

'You coming or not?' he asked impatiently.

'You're sure you wouldn't just like me to tail you and clear up the mess after you've had your little shoot out,' she said, referring to the events of the morning.

Dempsey looked at her sorrowfully. 'Oh come on. Give me a break. I've learnt my lesson, OK? I've already promised I won't go off on my own again. What more do you want me to say? I need you partner?'

Makepeace thought the matter over. She did so slowly and theatrically; much to the annoyance of Dempsey. 'Yes that seems to have a nice ring to it.'

'OK then. I need you partner. Now let's get our skates on.'

'Fools rush in where angels fear to tread,'

reminded Makepeace smugly. Dempsey scowled at her. She backtracked. 'Just a bit of partnerly advice.'

'Yeah well I don't want to be an angel,' snarled Dempsey. They rushed out of his apartment.

Chapter
SIX

The boys in records were as pleased with themselves as ever. Tracing photographs wasn't quite the same challenge as tracing teeth but when it ended in success, as it had done this time, it was almost equally as satisfying. The first thing they had discovered about the print was that it had been machine processed. It was eight-inch roll paper that had been cut up in a black-and-white printing machine with integral guillotine. The other important thing was the paper. It was Kentmere, stippled, grade three.

With these two pieces of information they looked through their records on commercial printers. There were only two that fitted the bill and the first one that they tried turned out to be the right one. The client had wanted a number printed up and they stuck in the memory of the technician who'd printed them for the very fact that they appeared to be surveillance photographs. The printers had been able to supply them with an address. It was a piece of good, honest police work and they were proud of it.

'What's the address?' demanded Dempsey, bursting into their office at speed with Makepeace trailing in his wake.

Arthur Wilson who'd been in charge of the operation, there being no teeth to trace that day, looked crestfallen. He'd expected to be embraced and congratulated on his sterling work. Instead he was confronted with Dempsey barking abrupt questions at him.

'Well we discovered . . .' He wanted to show off his department's ingenuity but Dempsey wanted none of it. He interrupted him.

'Wilson I don't have time for this crap. There's someone out there trying to kill me.' He waved his hand towards the window. 'I might have time to chew the cud about your monographs on cigarette ash and the tatoos of the Far East, later. But right now all I want to do is nail that woman out there before she nails me. Now give me that address.'

Wilson opened his mouth but nothing came out. He tried again, but again nothing. He'd never been spoken to like this before. He couldn't handle it. He held up the piece of paper with the address on like a house-trained zombie. Dempsey took it from him, read it and put it in his pocket.

'Great. Thanks. Good work.' He slapped the bemused Wilson on the back and swept out of the office again. Makepeace stayed for a moment, thinking that perhaps she ought to apologize to Wilson for her partner's brusqueness. But Wilson didn't look as if he'd really be able to take it in and, besides, she didn't want to lose Dempsey. She rushed out of the office after him.

* * *

Albert Ripley was fat and forty. His chin overlapped his shirt collar and made doing his top button up a bit of struggle. His one consolation in life was food. He was consoling himself at the present with a couple of spring rolls and a prawn curry which he hadn't yet started. He was a private investigator. He'd always wanted to be a private investigator until he'd become one. Then it became too late to get out and do anything else. He bit into his spring roll and a large lump of a greasy mixture of bean sprouts and God knows what else squirted out of the other end and landed in his lap. He cursed and grabbed a tissue out of the box on his desk. He got off as much as he could and threw the tissue at the waste-paper basket in the corner of the room. It was only a small room, about ten foot by ten foot, but he still managed to miss by about three foot. He made no move to pick it up. He looked down at his trousers again. They had so many stains on anyhow, that it was difficult to tell which was the new one.

The seediness of being a private investigator was part of what had attracted Albert Ripley into the profession. But he'd expected it to be a kind of glamorous seediness, not the seedy seediness that he had experienced. He had hoped for a life of car chases and complicated murder cases solved purely by his own brilliant reasoning. He'd expected too much. As it was he spent most of his time eating and his eating was financed by taking on jobs where he was little more than a peeping tom; trailing adulterous wives on behalf of manically jealous husbands and visa versa. He took another bite from his spring roll and wished that he'd become a train driver.

He stared out of his window, masticating slowly. The shambling roofscape of Bethnal Green stretched out before him. Some of the people who came up the six flights of stairs to his office used to ooh and aah over this weird collection of fire escapes, chimneys, sky-lights, drainpipes and oddly angled rooves. A major's wife, who suspected her husband of molesting young children, had once said that she found it very Dickensian. Albert Ripley found out, in turn, enough evidence to put the old man away for three years but the case never came to court as the old boy blew his brains out with the second barrel. Still, Ripley sometimes used the line about the roofscape looking Dickensian to impress other clients, so all was not lost. Himself, he hated the view; he found it intensely depressing.

He swallowed the spring roll that he'd been chewing. It had been a bad idea to chew it for so long. But he felt that he'd better try and make things last as he'd had no work for three weeks now. He kept looking in the papers and reading about growing crime figures but very little of it seemed to be coming his way.

Just then his front door flew open and Dempsey and Makepeace burst in. He looked up in surprise and in doing so he dropped the remains of his spring roll between his legs. From the manner of their entrance he could tell that Dempsey and Makepeace weren't the people from Littlewoods come to inform him of his good fortune. They had entered more in the manner of bailiffs or debt collectors. Whoever they were, Albert Ripley objected to them just bursting into his office without knocking. He leapt to his feet as fast as he could, as fast as it was possible for someone so grossly overweight. The remains of the spring roll fell to the floor. His chins shook with indignation.

'What the hell ...' But before he could get it out Dempsey interrupted him.

'Police,' he said, as if the word was a command. Ripley was lost for words. He looked from one to the other in amazement. One spoke in an American accent and the other was a woman. Who did they think they were fooling. He snorted in derision at Dempsey's claim.

'Huh — don't belive a word of it.'

Makepeace quickly produced her card and flashed it at him. She could tell that part of the reason that he didn't think that they were policemen was that she was a woman in plain clothes. She'd encountered that kind of bigoted attitude many times before but that didn't make it any better. Ripley bent down to peer at the card.

'I'm Sergeant Makepeace, he's Lieutenant Dempsey,' she added just in case he couldn't read. Ripley straightened himself up and inspected them again.

'From the local factory?' he asked with a note of disdain in his voice.

He obviously couldn't read thought Makepeace, SI 10 was stamped all over the card. Dempsey decided to clear the matter up. He didn't like men who felt that they were superior just because they called the local police station, the local factory. He flashed his badge also.

'SI 10,' he snarled 'and that's all you need to know.'

Ripley flopped back down into his chair casually, or as casually as a man so grossly overweight could manage. He leant back in his chair like a head master.

'I'll try hard, but I don't think I'm going to like you.'

Dempsey and Makepeace stared at him in disbelief. They hated him already and they were going to make no effort whatsoever to try and get to like him. The sooner they found out what they wanted to know and were able to get out of there the better. There was nothing about the man that one could like. There was a little to feel sorry for, but nothing to like.

'Private dick right?' sneered Dempsey. The phrase was completely appropriate. Dempsey glared at him and Ripley's bravado began visibly to crack. Makepeace took up the attack. She threw the photograph of Dempsey onto the desk in front of Ripley. He flinched away from the sudden movement.

'Ever seen this before?' she asked coldly.

Ripley leant forward and peered at the photograph. It had been his eyesight not his reading that had been at fault previously. He was able to focus on the photograph though. The obvious flicker of recognition flashed through his eyes. No wonder he had ended up in such squalid surroundings, thought Makepeace, he would probably have difficulty in taking candy from a baby. He would never have been much good at poker either, the blank face that he was trying to wear at the moment was as transparent as the emperor's clothes.

'Maybe,' he replied with a nonchalant shrug of his shoulders. Dempsey approached closer to the desk that Ripley was sheltering behind.

'No that's the wrong answer,' he said, enunciating each word threateningly. 'The game is "yes" or "no". I ask you whether you've ever seen this photograph before and you answer "yes" or "no". You think you can manage that?'

Ripley squirmed. The image he had of himself as the Philip Marlowe type tottered for a moment and then fell. He became the fat, pitiful, slob that he really was.

'You burst in here,' he complained 'I'm having my lunch — you don't even knock on my door ...' He trailed off.

Despite the pitiful nature of his protestations Dempsey and Makepeace didn't weaken. He'd brought upon himself everything that he was going to get and he deserved all that was coming to him. Dempsey dealt with the lunch complaint first, by chucking the remaining spring roll and the untouched prawn curry out of the open window. Ripley lunged after it to try and save his beloved food but he was too slow and too fat. He could only stand and watch. He looked like Tweedle-dee deprived of his brand new rattle. He sat down again in a sulk.

'Now,' continued Dempsey, 'you wanna follow your lunch?'

Ripley looked at him in amazement. He could tell that this wasn't just a kind gesture to a food lover. He looked across at Makepeace to protect him from this madman.

'Is he threatening me?' he asked her in threatened disbelief.

'I don't know.' She turned to Dempsey who was still glaring at Ripley. 'Are you threatening him?'

'Yes I am,' snarled Dempsey without moving.

Makepeace turned back to Ripley. 'Yes he is.' She sounded like a sales girl in a television advert, her voice sweetness and light.

Ripley made one last show of strength. 'Right I want my lawyer,' he said determinedly. He reached for the telephone. As he did so Dempsey calmly swept it off the desk, never taking his eyes off Ripley. Ripley bent down and began to grapple for it on the floor but his stomach made both bending down and grappling difficult processes.

Dempsey got to the phone before him and stamped on it. It was something that he'd been wanting to do for the last couple of days; take out his frustrations on the thing that was responsible for most of them. He ground the plastic under the heel of his boot. Ripley watched Dempsey's expression as he did so. He feared that all the anger and violence might soon be directed towards him as soon as Dempsey had made sure that the telephone was well and truly dead. He made a dash for the door. Dempsey saw him and pushed him back into his chair before his fat bulk had been able to build up any momentum.

'If you're looking for trouble Ripley — I'll help you find it,' warned Dempsey through clenched teeth.

'Now he can't say fairer than that, can he?' added Makepeace in her best television presenter's voice.

They both felt like they were a team again. Their argument was forgotten. Dempsey was the muscle. Makepeace was the needle. Ripley was beginning to get nervous. He thought that Dempsey was about to get violent and if there was one thing that he couldn't stand it was people getting violent, especially when he was on the receiving end of it. Dempsey clenched his right fist and Ripley tried to protect himself, verbally at first.

'You hit me, I've got a witness,' he warned. Dempsey looked around for the witness and then realized that Ripley meant Makepeace.

'Close your eyes, Harry,' he said casually. Makepeace made to do so and Ripley backed his chair away from Dempsey, but it was a small office and there was nowhere to hide unless he took Dempsey's advice and went to look for his lunch. Ripley cowered beneath an upraised flabby arm. Dempsey moved towards him menacingly.

'Now wait a moment,' Ripley held out his hand to ward him off, 'this is a diabolical liberty. I'm being harassed here ...'

No one was arguing with him. Dempsey snatched Ripley's arm away from his face and held it tightly, though not painfully. Things hadn't reached that stage yet. He put his face right up to Ripley's. Dempsey could smell his breath and he was no Violets MacGee, more like a Fu Man Chu.

'Last time around,' warned Dempsey, small sprays of spittle flying into Ripley's face. 'Have you seen this photograph?' Ripley made no answer. Dempsey squeezed his arm harder and asked the question again. 'Have you seen this photograph?' This time Ripley broke.

'Yes.'

Dempsey was glad to remove himself from his unpleasant proximity to spring roll stuck between browning teeth. He turned away from Ripley, who had begun to snivel, and addressed Makepeace. This was part of their well practised routine.

'Spying on and photographing an officer in pursuit of his duties, what's the sentence for that?'

Makepeace didn't need to answer. Ripley was already theirs.

'Look I didn't know that you were a cop,' he pleaded.

But Dempsey was not in a sympathetic mood, or, at least, that was the way that he knew he should behave from there.

'You believe him Harry?'

She shook her head as if she really wanted to believe him but just couldn't bring herself to do so.

111

Dempsey suddenly flashed his attention back to Ripley. 'Who did you take this photograph for?'

Ripley reacted as if from instinct; instinct or watching too many private detective films.

'Arr — well that's confidential see . . .'

Dempsey interrupted him by grabbing hold of his shirt collar and lifting him out of his chair. He could feel Ripley's chin enveloping his hand but he kept staring into Ripley's eyes. They were already frightened eyes. He made his other hand into a fist and showed Ripley a close up of it. Ripley got the message at last.

'Alright, there was a bird . . . a bird.'

Dempsey released him and he collapsed back down into his chair. 'Name,' demanded Dempsey.

'I don't know her name' he said, mopping his brow with a handkerchief that was obviously once white. 'It was all done on the telephone. It was a one off. They sent me the cash and I put the photographs in a packet and sent them to a general delivery address.

'Them?' asked Dempsey, somewhat surprised.

'Yeah well there weren't only that one.'

'How many were there then?'

'Oh scores of them. I don't know fifty, maybe more.'

'Fifty,' repeated Dempsey in disbelief. He looked across at Makepeace who was also taken aback by the information. They both hoped that that didn't mean that they'd have another fifty mornings like the last two mornings; fifty, maybe more.

They made their farewells, apologized about the accident with the telephone and left Ripley to his dirty little office, his depressing view and his miserable life.

The photograph had come to nothing after all. The only thing that their visit had achieved was to increase their fears. They looked for a silver lining but the only one that they could find was that they had been able to trace the photograph that far, which meant that one day they might be able to trace something else a little bit further. It hadn't been a mistake on her part, but it hadn't been perfect.

Chapter
SEVEN

Catherine Warren slid her key into the lock and twisted it slowly. The bolt slid smoothly back. It was well oiled. She slipped inside and closed the door behind her, pressing her back against it and breathing the atmosphere of the apartment deep into her lungs. She still found the experience very exciting. She felt that she had found her way into an inner sanctum and that here their souls could mingle just as their bodies had once done.

Dempsey very seldom came home at that time in the afternoon, she knew that from her observations. But if he did come back, well, too bad. She might kill him. She might make love to him. She might do both. She didn't know. He'd betrayed her but it was in her power to punish him or forgive him; to kill him or to let him live.

She wandered into the living-room brushing her hands caressingly over the surfaces. She picked up Dempsey's book which he'd left lying on top of a chest of drawers. She made a note of where he'd read to and put the book down in a slightly different position to the one that she'd found it in. She did this deliberately; after all he was a detective and ought to be able to spot things like that. She sat astride his gym equipment. She rubbed her hands across the leather seat and pressed her face against the cold metal of the weights. She pulled the bar that hung above her. He'd put on more weights. She liked strong men. She picked up Dempsey's workout towel that lay on the floor by where she sat and buried her face into it, breathing in the sweet aroma of Dempsey's body. She surrendered herself to him completely.

She pulled the towel off suddenly and flung it to the floor. She'd sensed herself beginning to weaken. She mustn't allow herself to do that. She felt that it had been weak of her not to dispose of him earlier that day in the school. She'd heard the shotgun blast and she'd also heard his retaliatory shots. He was obviously getting nervous, frightened even. She felt that it was only fair that she should frighten him a little before she killed him. She liked the idea that now he would be thinking of her almost all the time. His last thoughts at night would be of her and his first in the morning. It was almost like being married to him.

She wandered into the kitchen and spotted the lilies that she'd sent him. For a moment she was angry that he hadn't bothered to put them in water, but then she thought again and realized that it would be rather poetic if the lilies were to die with him. She examined them more closely; they were already starting to droop. Dempsey didn't have long to go. She turned on the kettle to make herself a cup of coffee. She looked around for a cup and in doing so noticed that the sink was full of washing up. She decided that she'd be helpful and do it for Dempsey. Again it made her feel like his wife. She liked the feeling.

But, almost as soon as she'd begun, she came across the cup that Makepeace had drunk her coffee out of. She didn't know that it had been Makepeace but she knew that it had been a woman from the lipstick ring around the rim. She stared at it blankly, her mind racing but her face betraying nothing of her emotions. The balance tilted. There was no chance now that she could forgive Dempsey. She suspected that he had been unfaithful to her and now she had the proof. She must kill him in order to save him. She smashed the polluted coffee-cup against the tap and watched as the pieces fell through the water to the bottom of the washing-up bowl. She stopped doing the washing up. She was his lover not his wife; his lover and his saviour.

She walked back into the living-room and stared out of the window. She looked across at her own window, there was no one in her flat. She gazed up and down the road, their road. The neighbours were nosey. They could well have seen her there but they didn't and she wouldn't have cared if they had done. She wanted the whole world to know about their love for each other. It was the only true and enduring thing in her life and it would be the only true and enduring thing after they were both dead. She glanced quickly across at her own flat to try and catch herself watching, but she'd gone somewhere.

She wandered back into the centre of the room, rubbing herself against the walls and furniture like a cat. Having marked out her territory, she made her way along the hall to Dempsey's bedroom. She checked in there for signs of another woman but she could find none. She entered the bathroom to do the same. She was glad that he'd cleaned it up. Finding no signs in the bathroom either she felt at ease again. Maybe the other woman hadn't penetrated the inner sanctum of the inner sanctum but that still didn't let Dempsey off. She re-entered the bedroom, flung the duvet off his bed and threw herself onto the mattress. She wallowed there for a moment, rubbing her hands across the sheets on which he'd lain only some seven hours previously. She kissed the pillow on which he'd rested his head. She looked around the room casually and suddenly started up at the sight of the open blinds. She rushed over to them and closed them. The neighbours were nosey. She didn't want any of them to know about their secret love. She didn't even want to let herself see.

The drawing of the blinds threw the room into a delicious dusk. Catherine Warren walked over to Dempsey's full length mirror and began to admire herself in it. Looking at herself now it didn't surprise her that Dempsey loved her with such a passion. She was the most beautiful woman that she'd ever seen. She kicked off her shoes seductively and began to unzip the zip that ran from the top to the bottom of her grey jump suit. She tantalized herself in the mirror. She pulled the suit first from her left shoulder and then from the right, each time caressing the smooth white flesh as if she were being undressed by, and undressing, someone else. She wasn't wearing a bra. She let her jump suit drop to the floor and stepped out of the crumpled ring of material. She admired her naked body in the mirror from every angle. She felt that she was irresistible. She moved towards Dempsey's bed and slid across his mattress. Just as she did so the front door of Dempsey's apartment rang.

Catherine Warren froze for a moment but neither her face nor her body revealed any signs of panic. She got off the bed and put on the robe that hung on the back of Dempsey's bedroom door. She made her way along the hall towards the front door. She didn't know who it was who had rung the front door and she didn't really care. She doubted that it was Dempsey, but if it were she might condescend to make love to him before she killed him. If it was the woman who had left the lipstick on the coffee-cup then she'd grab a knife from the kitchen and cut her head off. If it was someone else . . . well she'd just have to see.

She opened the door. It was someone else. It was Foley. He was holding up a black jacket in a polythene sleeve. It had just come back from the cleaners. Catherine Warren smiled at Foley as if he were an old friend.

'Ah, Mr Foley,' she addressed him as if he were one as well. Foley was slightly taken aback by this scantily clad young woman hailing him as if he were an old friend. He was old certainly but he couldn't remember ever having seen her before.

'Yes,' he said defensively, as if she was about to reveal that she was, in fact, Eamon Andrews. She was pleased with his reaction. She had the upper hand and she enjoyed that feeling.

'You see you're famous already,' she said.

'I am?' Foley was completely bemused by now, first she knew his name and now she thought that he was some kind of celebrity. He suspected a practical joke.

'Jim's told me all about you,' she explained.

Foley suddenly understood. 'Oh that's nice,' he said half heartedly, trying to muster a smile. He wondered why Dempsey had been talking to a pretty young woman about him. He reckoned that he must have been pretty stuck for conversation. He looked Catherine Warren up and down with his large watery eyes. He could tell that she had nothing on underneath the robe. The thought excited him. He tried to imagine, as he couldn't remember. She enjoyed him ogling her. She shifted from one foot on to the other and in doing so the belt of the robe loosened to the point where it was open right down to her belly button. Foley's eyes looked as if they were about to pop out of his head. He swallowed dryly and noisily. He tried to take his mind off his thoughts by thinking of Mrs Foley instead but he still couldn't remember anything about her.

Catherine Warren decided that she was tired of toying with this lecherous old man. She'd got all the enjoyment out of him that she could. She pulled the two sides of her robe together primly and interrupted his reverie.

'Yes?' she asked arrogantly, deliberately throwing cold water on his thoughts. Foley became flustered at her sudden change in attitude.

'. . . er . . . his jacket came back from the cleaners.' He thrust the jacket out towards her, to erect some kind of screen between them and protect him from the temptations of the flesh. She took the jacket from him, brushing her fingers against his.

'Oh it's his black jacket,' she said, as if it were almost a long lost friend as Foley had been previously. 'That's my favourite. Did they do a good job?'

Foley looked at her as if she were a nutter. He wasn't very good at hiding his feelings. He thought that all Americans were nutters, though. Still this one really was a bit much; thinking that he would have had a look to see if the dry cleaners had done their job properly — what did she think that he was paid for?

'I didn't look,' he replied aloofly.

'He always has "clean and retexture",' she told Foley, pretending that she thought he might be interested, but really to prove to herself, and to Foley, how

119

well she knew Dempsey. She was also proud of all the minor detail that she had dredged up with her research work.

'I'll just hang this up for him, thank you very much.' She tried to sound as if she was his wife.

'Pleasure,' smirked Foley. Her robe had begun to come loose again when she had taken the jacket from him. He grinned like a Cheshire cat. She shut the door abruptly in his face but the smile remained all the way back to his boiler room.

She walked back along the hall to the bedroom and hung up the jacket in Dempsey's wardrobe. She wondered whether he'd find it surprising to open the door and suddenly find it there. She thought not, as Foley had a master key to his apartment and would have probably hung up the jacket there anyway if she hadn't been there. She slipped the robe from her shoulders again and slid back onto the bed, this time pulling the duvet over her as well.

She closed her eyes and luxuriated in the sensuous touch of the soft warm cotton. She tried to imagine Dempsey in there with her. His firm muscular body, his ... but all that she could think of was Foley's leering face. He'd ruined it for her. She blamed him entirely. She'd forgotten about her own enjoyment at toying with him. She closed her eyes again and tried to think of Dempsey. She squirmed around, occasionally letting out sharp, breathy, erotic cries but always the image of Foley returned to haunt her.

She gave up. She swung her legs out of bed and walked over to the full length mirror. It seemed to her that she'd grown old in the last ten minutes. The beauty of the body had fallen from her. Her skin, previously smooth as marble, had become like an elephant's. Her body, previously perfectly proportioned, had begun to bulge and sag. She was old, ugly and no longer desirable. She blamed Dempsey.

She dressed quickly, drew the blinds and left the bed as much like she had found it as possible. She went back to the kitchen and cleared the broken cup out of the washing-up bowl, hiding the broken pieces in the bottom of Dempsey's dustbin bag. She took a new mug out of the cupboard and kissed the rim of it placing her familiar lip print on it. She placed the mug in the washing-up bowl. She wondered if Dempsey would notice the difference. She doubted it. She doubted if he'd notice that anything had changed. All he would know was what he heard from Foley and she doubted whether Foley would be able to give a very good description of her, or of her face at least.

She looked round the apartment one more time to check whether she'd left any too obvious pointers. She made her way towards the door. Before she left she took one last lungful of the air in Dempsey's department, like a pearl diver about to enter the murky depths. She sneaked out of the door and locked it quietly behind her.

She made her way home, satisfied with her afternoon's entertainment. She'd left a few clues for him to follow up, the most important of which were her fingerprints. Of course her fingerprints had been all over Dempsey's apartment for weeks now and they'd still not traced her, but she sensed that the big showdown might be coming soon. She reckoned that she'd really given him chance enough. It shouldn't be too difficult for him to find her now.

'He's in a difficult position,' said Makepeace evasively.

Spikings was quizzing her about Dempsey.

'Aren't we all,' he replied raising his eyes to the heavens and his superior's office on the floor above. 'What I want to know is how *you* think he is?' Spikings now fixed her with those large dark eyes of his set deep in the flesh of his face.

'Well, he seems to be fine — outwardly.'

'And inside?'

'Hard to tell. He plays it close.' Makepeace lied. She *did* feel that inside that rough exterior Dempsey *was* a little nervous and on edge, in fact she knew so, and had even seen physical manifestations of it. But she wasn't about to tell Spikings. She hadn't told him about the school incident either. She was a loyal partner.

'A copper who's never scared is a bad copper,' philosophized Spikings 'You question him about his . . . er . . . love life?' He spoke the words 'love life' as if they had a taste that disagreed with his palate.

'He says there's no one.'

'You believe that?'

'I believe that he thinks that there's no one.' Makepeace replied cagily.

'But you think that there's someone who he's overlooked?'

'Well it's the only explanation that I can think of.' Spikings nodded. It was the only plausible one that he could think of as well. He didn't like the idea of the *crime passionnel,* but he liked it even less when the two people involved were an SI10 officer and a high-powered-rifle-toting madwoman.

'Stick close to him Harry,' he ordered. 'Try and spend as much time with him as possible.' She nodded her agreement and he dismissed her.

When she re-entered the central office Dempsey

was tidying his desk. It didn't seem to be getting much tidier. He seemed to be shuffling things and pushing them from one side of the desk to the other. The top of the desk was becoming just visible though, so he was obviously making some headway. She walked over to him and stood by his desk. She wondered how close Spikings had meant by 'close' and what his interpretation of 'possible' was. Dempsey looked up and saw her standing there.

'You two been talking about me, then?' he asked.

'You know me, I can't talk about anything else.' She sat down on the corner of her own spotlessly clean desk.

'Oh I know that, but don't tell me that Spikings is fresh on me as well.'

'Only in an avuncular kind of way.'

'You mean he's going to offer me sweets and take me for a ride in his Daimler — I've always wanted a ride in that car.'

Makepeace became serious. 'I mean that he's concerned when one of his team seems to be retreating into their own personal little world and won't let anyone else in on it.'

Dempsey looked worried. 'You didn't tell him about the school outing, did you?' he asked anxiously. Makepeace smiled at his sudden change of mood.

'What, snitch on the Lone Ranger? What kind of yellow-bellied pinko do you think I am?'

Dempsey brushed aside her flippancy. 'Well what were you two talking about in there then?'

'You. I've told you.'

'Yeah, but what about me?'

'Well he was suggesting that we should get married and I asked him if he'd be best man. I wasn't jumping the gun was I?'

'Ha, ha.' Dempsey wasn't amused. Makepeace saw this and as she didn't want him to be in a sulk for the rest of the day, she told him the truth.

'All he said was that I should keep an eye on you?'

'Keep an eye on me?' he echoed blankly.

'Yeah stick as close to you as possible,' explained Makepeace, hoping that if she had to stick close to him he wasn't going to stay this dumb all the time.

She needn't have worried; the message soon got through to Dempsey as did the various interpretations of the words 'close' and 'possible'.

'Really?' His eyes widened with exaggerated lechery.

'I'm afraid so.' She narrowed her eyes in reply. Dempsey pondered a moment before speaking again.

'So,' he said suavely, 'do you fancy coming back to my place this evening?'

Chapter
EIGHT

Dempsey strolled into 'Nathan Detroit's' alone. The place had only opened about five minutes previously, so there were very few people in there. But one of them was Catherine Warren.

Dempsey went there quite often. It was quite close to the 'shop' and pretty good value. But the main thing that recommended it to Dempsey was that it served the best American hamburger he'd found in London, and on top of that it was the only place, apart from the occasional grossly over-priced brasserie, that served his favourite American lager. Of course the burgers weren't quite as good as the real McCoy and the lager seemed to taste rather different, having been shipped all the way over here. But it was as close as Dempsey had been able to get in London. The waitresses were really friendly too. They were American and they weren't surly and resentful like Dempsey found most British waitresses. He wondered if it was because they were paid better.

Dempsey walked up to the bar and leant over to grab the copy of *The New York Times* that they always saved for him, so as he could keep up with what was going on on the other side of the Atlantic. He groped for it, but couldn't find it. Paula, one of the waitresses working behind the bar, came to the rescue and found it for him. He thanked her and went to sit down at his normal table. He paused for a moment before opening the paper. Partly because he didn't dare look and see how his basketball team, 'The New York Knickerbockers', had got on, they were having an abysmally embarrassing season, and partly because for the first time that day he felt safe and secure. In there he found it hard to believe that the events of the last two days had really happened. Everyone around him seemed to be quietly content. It didn't seem that homicidal maniacs could exist in such a world. Later on in the evening the place got rowdier as it was invaded by hoardes of teenagers trying to emulate their heroes from *Animal House*. But even then the world only seemed to be Parental Guidance material. People weren't getting their brains blown out at bus stops.

Dempsey turned to the sports pages and scanned through the results column. He dropped the paper onto his lap in disgust. They'd lost again. He steeled himself to read about the ignomy of losing 112-93 to the Milwaukee Bucks. Seeing him lifting his paper up again Catherine Warren approached him. She wanted to give him a surprise.

'Hi Jim,' she said cheerfully. But Dempsey had heard her approach and wasn't surprised.

'Hiya Cath. How ya doing?' he asked equally cheerfully, glad not to have to think about the appalling recent form of his team. He was beginning to feel that it was him looking at *The New York Times* so eagerly after every match that was making them lose. He smiled up at her, wondering how many British waitresses would come up to their customers and greet them with a 'Hi Jim'. Meanwhile she was composing an answer to his question.

'Oh OK I suppose. How about you?'

Dempsey smiled again. He wondered what she'd say if he told her all that had happened to him over the last two days. She read his thoughts and smiled also. She was in the superior position once more.

'Well you know how it is,' he replied trying to weigh up his present situation. 'Life is hard . . .'

'And then you die,' interrupted Cath. Then laughed, half at her own joke and half at Dempsey's slightly surprised expression. 'I got to work late tonight,' she continued, 'one of the other girls has got flu.'

'Yeah?' said Dempsey. He wasn't at all sure why she was telling him this.

'But I'm off at eight . . .'

Dempsey interrupted. He realized what she was getting at and he wasn't at all keen.

'Sorry I've got someone joining me.'

'Why? Are you coming apart?' she retorted quickly, though the tone of her voice gave no hint that it was supposed to be a joke. Dempsey took it as one, all the same. He just assumed that her timing and delivery were bad.

'If vaudeville ever comes back you'll go a long way,' he replied. She'd already given him his complimentary glass of water but what he really wanted was a glass of beer to wash it down with or even better to replace it. Cath seemed to read his thoughts.

'And meanwhile how about a beer?'

Dempsey grinned. 'I thought you'd never ask.'

'The usual?'

'The usual.'

Dempsey followed her with his eyes as she went up to the bar to collect his beer. She'd made a positive effort to try and remember what kind of beer he liked to drink, that was America for you, he thought to himself. He looked around the restaurant again. It was beginning to fill up with those coming out of their offices for a quick drink with their mates at work before going back to their mates at home. A feeling of warmth for the rest of humanity suddenly swept through Dempsey. He picked up the paper again. He reckoned that the Milwaukee Bucks must've had a pretty hot team.

Makepeace entered. She looked around the restaurant as if she had only just reached eighteen and it was the first time she had been into an establishment where you could buy alcohol over the counter. The real reason for her wariness was that she hadn't really known what to expect from what Dempsey had described as his 'favourite haunt.' The name, 'Nathan Detroit's' had summoned up images of characters in wide-bodied suits eating apple-strudel washed down with prohibition liquor. As it was, the place seemed to be a curious amalgam of different kinds of Americana, mostly the healthy and youthful ones. It wasn't her kind of place; not that she wasn't still young and healthy, it was just that she preferred places that were a little more reserved. Still, she had to stick with Dempsey and this was his 'favourite haunt'. The proprietor switched on a video player and ten television sets burst into life blasting out directions to ten sets of fuzzy looking wide receivers and offensive line men. The proprietor turned down the sound, so as the commentary was only just audible over the hum of the traffic. Dempsey saw Makepeace approaching and folded up his paper.

She reached his table. 'So this is where you rush to when the sun goes down.'

'Yeah this is my joint,' he said proprietorially, with a large sweep of his hands.

'You're accent's grown thicker,' pointed out Makepeace.

'Yeah well when in Rome . . .'

'Well I'm glad that we didn't agree to meet in an Italian espresso bar then. I'd hate to hear your Latin.'

'Actually I speak Italian rather well,' said Dempsey indignantly. 'I used to have quite a few dealings with the mafia back in New York. Al Capone's nephew once congratulated me on my accent.'

'Oh really.' Makepeace didn't believe a word of it. 'Well let's hear a little snatch of it then.'

'Well it's mostly Sicilian dialect so I doubt that you'd understand it,' backtracked Dempsey.

'Try me.'

'OK.' Dempsey paused to re-arrange his mouth to really do justice to the Sicilian dialect. 'Uno espresso per favore.' He said in *Carry-on*-style Italian.

Makepeace wasn't finding his jokes very funny that day. She sneered at him. 'Great. Almost bilingual. Let's go.' She made to stand up but Dempsey prevented her.

'I'm afraid that I'm waiting for a beer. Don't you want something to eat or something?'

'No thanks, not before a workout.'

'OK. But you'll be missing out. They do the best hamburgers in Britain in this place. Not as good as the American ones of course, but close. The beer's good too. America's finest.'

'You sound as if you're getting homesick,' said Makepeace, slightly surprised.

'Well don't you ever get homesick, muscle-man?'

'You have to leave home to get homesick.'

Dempsey laughed at her answer. 'Hey you must be a detective or something. Well don't you ever get sick of being home all the time then?'

'Yeah. That's why I'm redecorating my place.'

'Don't be evasive. Don't you ever get sick of being in the same town in the same country all the time?'

Makepeace thought for a moment. 'No not really.' Dempsey shrugged

'Well that's the end of that one then isn't it?' He turned and shouted to Cath who was still standing at the bar staring at them. 'I'm waiting for a beer over here.'

Cath smiled back at him politely, though there was a hint of anger in her eyes. 'Coming up.'

'I don't think that you should be drinking just before a workout,' advised Makepeace rather prudishly.

'Who said I was working out? It's you who's doing the workout I'm just going to stand around and shout out encouragement.'

Cath arrived with the beer. Dempsey took a large gulp and smirked at Makepeace, his top lip covered in froth. Cath handed Makepeace her complimentary glass of water. She'd heard what they'd just been talking about. She'd heard that Dempsey was going to give Makepeace a workout. She tried to keep the anger bottled up inside. She threw Makepeace a rather saracastic smile and Makepeace smiled back superciliously. Dempsey caught this interchange. He interpreted it as just a clash of very different characters. He decided to introduce the two of them, knowing that they wouldn't get along at all.

'Oh by the way this is Cathy, another American — Harry — Harry, Cathy.'

They nodded to each other apprehensively. Makepeace wasn't used to being introduced to waitresses and Cathy wished that she had had the presence of mind to carry some kind of poison with her for just such a moment. Having none to hand, she clumsily reached forward to reposition the flowers on the table and in doing so knocked Makepeace's complimentary glass of water into her lap.

Makepeace grabbed the glass and jumped to her feet. Cathy started apologizing almost before the glass had begun to fall.

'Oh God I'm sorry . . .' She made a move to try and help wipe some of it off but Makepeace prevented her.

'It's OK,' she said. But her tone of voice implied that it wasn't really OK at all, it was just that she didn't want her discomfort compounded by people creating a scene as well. Dempsey recognized a well known, and often encountered, British trait.

'You trying to get a bigger tip or something?' asked Dempsey, a little annoyed with Cathy.

'No this comes with the service.' She was trying the vaudeville routine again but it worked even less well than the previous one. It was far too soon after her slapstick performance.

Dempsey drank the rest of his beer quickly and left with Makepeace who was impatient to get on with the workout. Dempsey didn't say good-bye to Cathy, not because he was annoyed with her, but because she appeared to be serving other people and wasn't looking in their direction when they left. Cathy did see them leave, however. She had kept her eyes on them all the time, and particularly on Makepeace. She watched them leave in the mirror above the bar and as soon as the front door had closed behind them, she broke off from the couple whom she was serving to watch them through the window. The couple protested as they were in the middle of making up their order so she flicked them a V-sign which seemed to shut them up temporarily. She watched as Dempsey and Makepeace got into their separate cars and Makepeace followed his out of the car park. Cathy ripped off her apron in disgust and threw it onto the floor. Now she had two people to kill.

She strode into the back of the restaurant, changed quickly back into her everyday clothes and handed in her notice to the proprietor. He was too bemused by her seemingly irrational and unprovoked behaviour to even speak, let alone try and prevent her. As she left she could hear the couple that she'd been serving protesting weakly.

When she got home, before she opened her door, she checked to see if anyone had entered her flat while she had been away. No one had, the hair that she'd stuck with saliva between door and frame was still there. She unlocked the door, went inside and turned on the living-room light. Her apartment was far smaller than Dempsey's. Her living-room was her kitchen and dining-room as well. Her bedroom was minute and she only had a shower, no bath, even though they still called it a bathroom. As for her personal touches there were none, apart, that is, from Ripley's photographs of Dempsey.

They were plastered all over the living-room walls. Ripley had been right when he'd said that there might be more than fifty of them, a hundred was nearer the mark. Some of them already bore that familiar bright-red lipstick print. In others Dempsey had had his eyes either poked out with some sharp object or scribbled out with a biro. Others had obscene and perverted graffiti scrawled across them. Only a few remained untouched. Cathy took down one of these and tore at it until it was no more than confetti. But it made her feel no better about seeing Dempsey with *her* in the place where she herself had first met him. She felt there was something disgusting about it. She walked over to the window and looked across at Dempsey's apartment. The bedroom blinds were open but the living-room curtains had been drawn.

She would have to resort to the bugs. She'd installed a number of bugging devices about a week ago on another afternoon visit to Dempsey's apartment. There were two in the living-room, one in the kitchen, one in the bedroom and even one in the bathroom. The one in the bathroom she found quite amusing but that kind of thing didn't really turn her on. She hadn't had much opportunity to use them, as yet, as Dempsey spent a great deal of time out and in the last week hadn't had anybody in his flat while she had been listening, apart from Foley. She had listened to him pacing around the house and once she'd heard him working out, but this was the first real and important test for her system. She walked over to the receiver, which was on the table by the chair from which she could watch Dempsey's window in comfort, and switched it on. The receiver was a black box about a foot square with a speaker, an aerial, a tuning knob and a number of other knobs that enabled one to call up pre-set frequencies. She switched to the living-room bug nearest the gym equipment. Dempsey's voice came through loud and clear.

'Try and keep your back straight, don't arch.'

Cathy sat back to listen but she was unable to listen comfortably.

'Try and keep your back straight, don't arch.'

Makepeace pulled her stomach in and pushed back her shoulder blades. Dempsey wasn't annoying her yet but she could tell that he might be building up to it. As soon as she'd arrived she'd changed out of her wet skirt and into her leotard, pulling a sweatshirt over the top of it. Dempsey had said that it was best to start off with not too much weight, but really he'd put on so little that pushing it up and down was no more exhausting than pushing a pen. She knew that he'd done this deliberately. He knew how much she objected to being thought of as a weak woman. She wasn't a weak woman, of course, she was stronger and fitter than most men. Still, she felt that with the life she led, the stronger and fitter she was the better. She was doing an exercise that involved sitting astride the seat of the largest part of the mini gym and pulling a weighted bar down from head height to shoulder height alternatively front and back. She wasn't even working up a sweat.

'Yeah that's good,' encouraged Dempsey. He'd also changed into his workout clothes, so as Makepeace wouldn't feel awkward, but he didn't intend to do any of the exercises.

'Now bring it down the front,' he said unhelpfully. Makepeace pulled the weight down to her chest. It was even easier that way. She let the weights pull the bar back up to arm's length and then pulled it down again until it touched against her shoulder blades.

'Alternate front and back,' repeated Dempsey, feeling rather redundant but enjoying the sight of

Makepeace pumping iron in his front-room. He decided that he'd try and explain the science of weightlifting to her.

'You see this way you work the complimentary muscle groups.' He gestured to try and illustrate what he meant by complimentary muscle groups but pulled his hands back because by complimentary muscle groups he really meant Makepeace's deltoids and her breasts, or more accurately her pectorals, and he thought that it was really too early for such detailed discussion.

Makepeace rested the weights above her head for a moment. She didn't like the way that he was smirking to himself. She was determined to take the whole thing seriously.

'I think that I could do with some more weight,' she said matter-of-factly.

Dempsey stopped smirking and repositioned a pin so as to double the weight that Makepeace was lifting.

'Try that.'

Makepeace tried it. That was better. It was hard and it hurt but Makepeace felt that that must mean that it was doing her some good.

'That's better.' She gritted her teeth and pulled the weight down to her chest again. Sweat sprang up her brow. Dempsey looked on admiringly.

'Okay.'

Catherine Warren, meanwhile, was definitely not feeling OK. If the living-room curtains had not been drawn she would have blown them both away already. But as it was she was impotent. Impotent but mad as hell. She paced up and down the room like a caged animal, pausing occasionally to slash at one of the photographs of Dempsey, with a six-inch knife. She too had noticed the note of suggestion in Dempsey's voice. There was no chance of forgiveness now. Makepeace wasn't even an American. It wasn't right and it wasn't fair. She stuck a drawing pin into Dempsey's brain.

'OK well I think that that's enough for that particular muscle group,' said Dempsey after Makepeace, to his amazement, had done fifty of the previous exercise and looked as if she was easily capable of doing fifty more. 'I think that the next muscle group that we should concentrate on, is the thighs and stomach.' He moved over to the other piece of gym equipment with weights. 'Not that there's anything wrong with your thighs or stomach, of course,' he added to annoy her.

Makepeace duly scowled at him. But by doing so she was only encouraging him.

'You know we could make this a regular thing two or three times a week,' he suggested.

'Well I think that once is quite enough for me,' replied Makepeace tartly. 'Anyhow I'm joining a gym next week.'

Dempsey looked up at her in amazement. 'Why join a gym when you can join here for free? I'll throw in the personal tuition for nothing.' He sounded like someone on the china stall at the market.

'It's the personal tuition I'm worried about.'

Dempsey took the hint and began to explain the next exercise very impersonally and objectively. He was interrupted by the telephone. They both looked at each other apprehensively. The moment that it had started ringing they had both been reminded of all that had happened to them over the last couple of days. Even if it turned out to be Spikings, ringing up to be avuncular, the moment of forgetfulness had gone.

Dempsey moved towards the phone, though he felt like letting Makepeace answer it like last time. His hand hovered for a moment over the phone. He almost felt that if *he* picked it up, then it was bound to go dead on him but if *she* picked it up, then there was bound to be someone else on the other end. He told himself not to be so babyish and picked up the phone. But before he put it to his ear he cupped his hand over the mouthpiece.

'Are you here?' he whispered across to Makepeace. She shook her head. He thought that she looked worried as well. He was glad that she was there. Dempsey put the phone to his ear.

'Yo, Dempsey.'

The phone went dead and the dialling tone echoed once again in his ear. He threw the phone back onto the hook. The phone calls weren't so much frightening him as making him angry and frustrated. He was reminded of the game everybody used to play when they were kids, of ringing front door bells and running away before the person came to the door. This time, however, he was on the receiving end and no matter how fast he picked up the phone he wouldn't be able to catch whoever was on the other end. Nor was this a game. The person on the other end of the line had already killed one person. Dempsey tried to remember the name. Basset, that was right, Theodore Basset.

Makepeace watched him intently, she could tell that the phone calls were starting to get to him. They weren't going to drive him mad but, if he wasn't careful, they might anger him into behaving rashly or dangerously. She tried to take his mind off them.

'So how do I use this one?' she asked.

Dempsey explained it to her readily. He too knew that it was bad for him to dwell on the calls. He didn't want to give the caller that feeling of satisfaction.

'OK. Well you put your feet underneath those pads. Lift your legs slow ... don't lock your knees ... now let it release to a count of four.' Makepeace followed his instructions attentively and accurately. 'Right, it works the trapeze here,' Dempsey pointed. 'That's good, do a hundred of those.'

He walked across to the exercise that Makepeace had started on, adjusted the weight and grabbed hold of the bar.

'I think that I might pump iron myself, after all.' He pulled the bar down to his chest and let it rise back up again gradually. He stared straight ahead, automaton-like, gritting his teeth.

Makepeace paused for a moment to look across at him. He didn't seem to notice that she'd stopped. She decided that Spikings was right, he definitely did need a bit of looking after.

Cathy had enjoyed the telephone call immensely. Though Dempsey and Makepeace hadn't discussed it between themselves, she could tell from their reactions, both as soon as it started ringing and when she put her end down, that she was really getting to Dempsey. She had stuck the knife in and now she was twisting it. She would have liked Dempsey to have been reduced to swearing down the phone but the element of nervousness that had entered his voice, even though he was trying to hide it, was satisfying enough at this stage in the proceedings. She listened in to the bugging device again. They had stopped talking and now all she could hear was them grunting and breathing as they continued with their exercises. She considered stopping them talking a minor victory but the real victory would only come when she had stopped them talking for ever.

Makepeace and Dempsey worked out for about another fifteen minutes. The only words passing between them being Makepeace's questions and Dempsey's answers about various bits of apparatus and types of exercise. Dempsey worked hard and determinedly. He was soon sweating profusely. Makepeace's heart hadn't really been in it ever since the phone call. She kept wanting to say something soothing to Dempsey but she couldn't find the moment or the words. Eventually she decided that it would be best to call it a day and leave him to work things out on his own, both physically and mentally. She sat up and swung her feet to the floor.

'I think I've had enough for the first time.'

Dempsey continued unabated. 'Sure, you want to have a shower?'

'Please.'

'Help yourself.'

'Thanks.' Makepeace walked off towards the bedroom.

This news excited Cathy. She grabbed the suitcase that contained the rifle out from under the bed and hurriedly began to assemble it. There was none of the ritual of last time. She fumbled and flustered. The rifle assembled, she darted back to the front window and looked out. Makepeace had entered the bedroom and was sitting on the bed taking off her training shoes. The blinds were still open. Cathy groped for a bullet from the box on top of the television set and crammed it into the firing mechanism. She slid it into position with the bolt but didn't yet bother to aim the rifle. She'd decided that she'd wait until Makepeace was totally naked before she killed her. That way her dead body would be more of a lesson to Dempsey.

Makepeace removed the towelling bands from her wrists and threw them onto the floor then she pulled her sweat shirt up over her head to reveal her sweat stained leotard underneath. Cathy opened the top half of the window and leant the barrel of the rifle on the top of the window frame. She adjusted the telescopic sight to make amends for the difference in distance between this shot and the last one. She took aim. Through the sight she was able to see Makepeace pull the straps of her leotard down over her shoulders. Before she took it off completely she walked over to the window. Cathy tightened her finger on the trigger. It was as if Makepeace was walking to the window to give her an easier shot. Her hand began to tremble with excitement. She went into her deep breathing and concentration routine again. She steadied herself and looked through the sight again. But when she did so everything seemed to have gone white. She cursed. Makepeace had gone to the window, not in order to give her an easier shot, but to draw the blinds. She was tempted to let fly a shot anyhow, but she stopped herself. Dempsey had deserved some kind of warning. She didn't.

Cathy drew her own curtains. There would be nothing else to see that night. She placed the rifle down against the inside of the window frame and cursed herself for not having the foresight to have kept it there always. If she had done so, half her work might already have been done. She switched over the receiver to the bedroom bugging device. But could hear nothing. She imagined Makepeace lounging seductively in Dempsey's bed, just as she had done previously that day. The image annoyed her. Makepeace had undressed on that hallowed ground where only she was allowed to do so.

She heard the shower start up in the bathroom and switched over to the bathroom bugging device. She'd never thought of having a shower in Dempsey's apartment herself. It suddenly seemed to her that not only was Makepeace a rival but that she was ahead of her because she'd had a shower. She switched over to the living-room bug again to make sure that Dempsey hadn't sneaked into the shower with her; all she was able to hear on the bathroom bug was running water. Dempsey was still pumping away at the weights, much to her relief. She listened for a moment to his grunting and groaning. It grew louder and louder as the weights felt heavier and heavier and as his arms became weaker and weaker. Cathy switched the machine back to the bathroom. Makepeace was still in the shower. Cathy was glad. She'd had an idea.

Makepeace luxuriated in the shower. The day had been a long and hard one for her as well as for Dempsey and now it was good to lose herself purely in the pleasures of the flesh for a moment. The feeling of the water pounding against her skin and gradually massaging her wrung-out muscles back to life went some of the way towards rejuvenating her. The grime and sweat of the day were being washed away to make way for the purity of the night. She closed her eyes and tried to think of nothing. But after about ten minutes the water begun to run cold. She dried herself quickly and dressed.

When she came back into the living-room, Dempsey was still exercising. By this time he was breathing like a horse and sweating like a pig, but he was still capable of human conversation.

'You off then?' he asked.

'Yes. Thanks a lot.'

'Anytime.'

'Don't overdo it.'

'Oh this is just a light workout for me.' He bent over and looked as if he might collapse. Makepeace moved forward to see if he needed help. He held out his hand to stop her. He didn't need help, he just needed air. 'Don't worry,' he said, sitting up and trying to breathe in a controlled way.

'Don't you worry either. We'll get her.'

'I know. See you tomorrow. Take care.'

'And you.'

Chapter
NINE

Makepeace left, closing the door quietly behind her. Outside it was a beautiful evening, warm and starry. An almost full moon flooded its cool blue light into the dark recesses left unlit by the orange street lamps. The combination of the two gave the street a surreal air. Makepeace paused for a moment before walking to her car. The whole world seemed quiet and at ease, as if after a sudden snow fall. The events of the morning seemed to have happened years ago. It appeared impossible to her, at that moment, that all the crimes and evils that she had encountered in her past could have ever really existed in a world that was also capable of producing evenings as beautiful as this one. She stopped herself before she got too carried away. She reminded herself that what she saw now was the illusion and it was her past that was the reality. She got into her car and drove home. The lights were against her all the way.

When she arrived back, her house was in chaos. It hadn't been searched or ransacked by vandals or anything like that. Far worse; the decorators had moved in. Sliding her key into the lock, Makepeace had dreaded to think what she might find inside. She was sure that they would have misunderstood her instructions and confused the colours for the paint-work and the walls. But she held back her feelings of despair until she was able to see what they had really done. She pushed open the door and switched on the light. They'd broken it. Typical she thought to herself, they'd probably banged against it with one of their ladders and hadn't bothered to check whether they'd broken it or not.

She picked her way through her living-room, or drawing-room as she called it. The furniture had all been moved and was covered in white dust-sheets in order to conceal its sharp protruding edges. The place looked as if someone had died in there. Fortunately the moon was shining brightly through the windows so the journey to the kitchen wasn't too hazardous. Makepeace made it and turned on the kitchen light. It was broken also. At first Makepeace assumed that it was just a fuse that had gone but then she looked across at the kettle. Its small red light still glowed. Then she remembered that the lights and the sockets had different fuses. She looked up at the kitchen bulb accusingly. Since she last looked at it her eyes had become more accustomed to the light. She now saw that it wasn't that the light was broken, the bulb had been removed completely. She glanced quickly back into the living-room. The bulb had been removed from there also. There was something strange going on.

She made her way back towards the front door,

hugging the wall as closely as possible. As she moved and her angle changed, she suddenly saw something flash in the darkness. It was a knife. Someone was standing in the darkness between the two windows; she could feel them now. She made a dash for the drawing-room door but the figure saw her moving and got there first. Makepeace jumped back to avoid the figure's lunging arm. The knife buried itself in the door six inches from Makepeace's heart. The figure wrestled desperately to try and remove the knife. Makepeace was able to see the silhouette against the moonlit front garden. The attacker was small and dressed entirely in black, right down to a black bala-clava. A Gurkha, thought Makepeace. She caught a whiff of perfume. It was the madwoman. It was Cathy.

Makepeace kicked Cathy's hand away from the knife. But the extra impetus provided by the kick enabled Cathy to come away still holding it. Makepeace grabbed for the knife hand and wrestled it to the floor. But Cathy was strong. She had the strength of the mad. She twisted like an eel and suddenly Makepeace found herself underneath her. Cathy moved the knife towards Makepeace's jugular, her whole weight pressing down on it. Makepeace tried to push her back desperately. She wished that she hadn't expended quite so much energy earlier that evening in Dempsey's flat. At least she hadn't done any bench presses. She did have a couple of advan-tages over her assailant though; she was bigger than her and she was saner than her. She brought her knee up into Cathy's side with all the strength of the desperate. Cathy was sent flying sideways, dropping the knife with the unexpected pain. Makepeace was closer to the knife and at this stage more on the

145

attack. She scrabbled for the knife but as she did so Cathy leapt to her feet and sprinted out towards the back of the house. Makepeace forgot about the knife and ran after her.

Cathy jumped through the dining-room french windows, through which she had initially entered the house, and leapt over the wall at the end of the back garden. Makepeace reached the french windows as Cathy leapt but she didn't bother to pursue her. She was too tired and, besides, she didn't like the idea of chasing a madwoman through the streets of London at that time of night. She listened to Cathy's footsteps running down the road, then slumped down on the dining-room floor.

She sat there, in the same position for about five minutes getting her breath back and trying to compose her mind. It had been an extra workout that she hadn't really needed. The moonlight shimmered through the trees, the shadows animating the dining-room wallpaper. Makepeace climbed to her feet painfully. The adrenalin had numbed the pain initially but, as the level died down, Makepeace realized that their fight had, in fact, been quite a bruising one. She made her way back into the drawing-room. She supposed that she ought to report in about her night visitor. She wasn't too keen on the idea of having all those boys from forensics traipsing around her house at that hour of the night, or at any hour of the night for that matter, but they might be able to come up with something useful.

She began searching for the telephone beneath the white sheets. She guessed that it would be about where she'd left it that morning. She approached a likely looking hiding place and as she did so the phone started to ring immediately from somewhere behind her. She turned and walked towards it. It was, of course, coming from the largest pile of her paraphernalia in the room. She got down onto her hands and knees and began to search for it. She found it after about the twelfth ring, hidden in an old hat-box of hers. She made a mental note to tear a strip off the decorators in the morning. She paused for a few seconds before answering it and made a silent wish that it was Dempsey. Then she could explain everything to him and he would go through all the hassle of phoning Spikings, the police, forensics, etc.

She picked up the phone. It was a pay phone. It could still be Dempsey but the odds were lengthening.

'Hello,' she spoke into it tentatively when the person at the other end had put their money in. It wasn't Dempsey. Her wish hadn't come true. Her knight in shining armour hadn't rung up just in time to save her from the unpleasantness of reporting another unsuccessful murder attempt. It was Cathy, the wicked witch, the attempted murderer herself. Her voice was a savage whisper.

'Hey bitch! Leave my man alone,' she snarled.

Makepeace remained calm. She'd just fought off this woman's attempts to cut her head off. She wasn't going to be frightened by a simple phone call. For a start it meant that she wasn't within striking distance. 'Who are you talking about?' she asked in her Henley regatta voice.

'Jim,' snapped back Cathy. 'Just get out of his life and stay out.'

The phone went dead.

The boys from forensics were a little slow arriving. They preferred criminals who kept regular hours.

Again they were disappointed not to find a corpse or a missing murder implement. They did however fingerprint everything in sight, even though Makepeace had told them that she was sure that her attacker had been wearing gloves.

She had phoned Dempsey right after Cathy's phone call and he'd come round at once. He'd been very comforting and, though she knew that he was worried by this turn of events, just as she was, she also felt that he was glad to have someone else to worry about. Now he didn't have to worry about himself all the time. At present he was sitting next to Makepeace on a sofa that they'd managed to extricate from beneath the sheets. They were both holding cups of coffee and looking on in some amazement at the antics of the boys from forensics. Dempsey turned to her.

'Are you sure you're alright?' he asked. His concern showed.

'Yeah fine. I'm just glad that I didn't do another ten sit-ups.'

'Did you get a look at her?'

'Only by moonlight and she was wearing a balaclava. She was about five-foot-two though, and slimly built.' She rubbed the bruises on her wrist. 'But strong.'

'Well I suppose that narrows the field . . . a little.'

Spikings suddenly emerged from the hall, for some obscure reason he'd come in through the back of the house, the way Cathy had fled.

'Too easy to break in here,' he remarked gruffly. 'Should have better security. You alright?' he asked Makepeace almost as an afterthought. She nodded. He was about to go upstairs and inspect the security up there when he noticed that Dempsey was still wearing his workout clothes.

'Good grief, what have you been up to at this time of night?' he asked.

'I've been working out,' replied Dempsey defensively.

'Working out what?' said Spikings, genuinely unaware of the phrase.

'Long division sums. What do you think?' said Dempsey aggressively. He turned his attention to Makepeace again. Spikings stood in the doorway watching him for a moment. He hoped that one of his best officers wasn't about to crack. He looked from Dempsey to Makepeace. He hoped that Dempsey's anxiety wouldn't communicate itself to her. He didn't want one of his best teams to crack up, either. He left to rattle a few windows upstairs.

'Did she speak?'

'What?' Makepeace didn't take in the question as she was anxiously watching one of the boys from forensics who was fingerprinting a particularly valuable piece of porcelain.

'Did you hear what her voice sounded like?'

'No she didn't say anything. She grunted a bit when I kneed her in the ribs but nothing to go on.'

'But she phoned you as well.'

'Yes but she whispered like last time.'

'What did she say?'

'She seemed to think that the two of us were going out together. Funny huh?'

'Yeah well she's always seemed to me to be a dame with a sense of humour.'

Makepeace leant back on the sofa. 'Well let's just hope that we get the last laugh.'

They both sat for a moment in thoughtful silence. It was broken by Arthur Wilson. He approached

Makepeace timorously.

'I wonder if I could take a sample from underneath your fingernails?' he asked. It wasn't really his job but he'd got lumbered with night duty as there was a bug going around the department. He'd known it wasn't his day when he'd had the encounter with Dempsey earlier. He knew it wasn't his night when he encountered him in the doorway of Makepeace's house.

Makepeace held out her hand obediently. She knew that there was nothing to find underneath her nails as she hadn't managed to dig them into Cathy's skin but it wasn't really worth arguing about it. Wilson took her hand nervously. He was aware that Dempsey was keeping a close eye on him. He scraped along the underside of the nails with a small metal instrument specially designed for the purpose. He held a piece of paper beneath, in order to catch anything that he managed to scrape out. It looked a strange manicure. Nothing fell out, of course. Makepeace's nails were quite long but she kept them scrupulously clean and she'd only very recently had a shower. Wilson scrumpled up the piece of paper and apologized. As he walked away he reflected that he much preferred taking fingernail samples from the dead.

After about another five minutes of slopping graphite powder all over Makepeace's most valuable ornaments, the forensics boys made their farewells and left. Everyone was glad to see them go. Dempsey and Spikings stayed on to try and persuade Makepeace not to spend the night there. Spikings recommended a hotel and Dempsey recommended his place. But Makepeace was adamant, and though they were adamant too, she was the most adamant. Eventually, at about three o'clock in the morning they both left and Makepeace locked the front door securely behind them.

She made her way up to her bedroom and locked herself in. She undressed and climbed into bed but, even though she was tired, she had great difficulty in getting to sleep. As she stared at the shadows that the moon cast on the ceiling and walls of her room, the smell of Cathy's perfume returned to her suddenly. She started up in her bed and glanced around the room. The door was locked and so was the window out onto the balcony. It was only to her memory that the smell had returned. But, smell being so volatile a thing, she thought that she had smelt it again, there, in her bedroom. It was a smell that she had smelt before the events of that evening. She concentrated her mind trying to remember where, but was unable to. But, just as she was drifting into sleep, it came to her. It had been in the perfume hall at Harrods. She laughed at her paranoia and tried to get to sleep again, but still there was something nagging at the back of her mind. She'd smelt that smell somewhere else as well. Only for a instant, but the memory of it was lurking somewhere in the dark recesses of her brain.

Dempsey didn't sleep well that night either. While Makepeace was trying to pinpoint the smell, he was trying to pinpoint the voice once more. But both of them were wasting their time. Their minds just span round in circles. In the end they both fell asleep. He dreamt of going back to school and she of returning home to find her house decorated entirely in luminous red. They say that some of the greatest scientific discoveries have been made through dreams but they didn't prove much help when it came to placing perfumes or voices.

Chapter
TEN

Dempsey and Makepeace arrived at the 'shop' almost simultaneously the following morning. They smiled at each other cheerfully across the car park.

'Good morning,' shouted Dempsey. It was, but neither of them felt as if it was.

'Morning,' responded Makepeace, trying to match him in gaiety of tone 'Sleep well?'

'Like a top. And you?'

'Like two tops.'

They entered the building and both poured themselves large cups of coffee. They sat down at their separate desks and drank thoughtfully. One man had been killed and now there had been an attempt on Makepeace's life and they were still no nearer their prey. The bullet and its casing had come to nothing, the lilies had come to nothing, the shotgun had come to nothing, the photograph had come to nothing, the knife left in Makepeace's house had come to nothing, in fact, everything had come to nothing. They both had a second cup of coffee. There didn't seem to be anything else that they could do. They were in the uncomfortable position of having to sit back and wait for the killer to make her next move.

Spikings leant out of his office and beckoned them both in. They had nothing else to do, so they went in. Spikings motioned to them to sit down.

'Well?' he asked, still standing himself.

'Well what?' asked Dempsey.

'What are we going to do?'

'There's nothing much that we can do at the moment,' answered Makepeace. 'Not until something else turns up.'

'There is one thing,' corrected Dempsey. He paused for a second in order to give dramatic impact to what he was about to say. 'You can take Harry off the case.'

'Makepeace turned to him in amazement. At first she was too surprised even to speak.

'Why should I do that?' asked Spikings, also taken back by Dempsey's request. Makepeace was beginning to recover from the initial shock.

'Because she's obviously in danger if she hangs around with me, that's why. You saw what happened last night.' Dempsey became heated.

'Well ...' considered Spikings.

'Come on!' shouted Dempsey in disbelief at Spikings' hesitancy. 'Harry gets wasted because some weirdo is trying to blow *my* brains out, how are you going to feel about that?'

This was too much for Makepeace. In some ways she liked the fact that Dempsey betrayed a protective attitude towards her on occasion. But not on this occasion. She knew that Dempsey didn't just want her off the case because it was dangerous, it was because she was a woman. Her tongue became untied. She unleashed it on Dempsey.

'Look if anybody should be taken off the case it's you,' she shouted.

'Don't be ridiculous,' snorted Dempsey. 'I *am* the

case ...' Spikings tried to intervene as peacemaker but his protestations went unheeded.

'You're the target,' corrected Makepeace.

Dempsey glared at her. 'Oh come on — some nut's trying to blow my brains out and you want to get in on it.'

Makepeace took a deep and despairing breath and drew herself up to her full height in order to deliver the *coup de grâce* but was prevented from doing so by a deafening noise. It was Spikings.

'Cut it out. Both of you,' he bellowed.

The whole of London seemed to fall silent for a moment. Even the roar of traffic faltered for an instant on hearing this rival roar from a mere mortal. Spikings seemed even to have startled himself. He paused to regain his composure. Someone started typing again in the central office. He turned to Makepeace.

'He's got a point you know Harry,' he said resignedly.

Makepeace slumped back down into her chair in disbelief. To her it seemed like a conspiracy to keep her inside, washing up the coffee cups, while the boys went outside to play with their guns. Dempsey had played a dirty trick on her; he'd appealed to Spikings' old world values of gentlemanly behaviour and the weakness of women. He'd appealed and his appeal had been heard. She turned to Dempsey scornfully.

'You devious bastard.' She spat out the words. Dempsey knew that she didn't really mean it.

'I love it when you talk to me that way.'

But this touching moment between them was interrupted by the telephone. It began to ring. Spikings snatched it up and barked into it gruffly, quite contrary to SI 10 policy.

'Who's that?' It was quite obvious that he'd never been a telephone receptionist. On hearing the voice at

154

the other end his face lit up with excitement. He smothered the mouthpiece with his hand.

'It's her,' he said eagerly. Dempsey and Makepeace looked less enthusiastic. They'd both spoken to her on the phone now and they were in agreement that she wouldn't make it on to any British Telecom adverts.

'She didn't by any chance say who she was under your subtle interrogation did she?' asked Dempsey unhopefully.

Spikings ignored him. He gestured to grab Makepeace's attention. 'Get a trace on this call,' he ordered. Makepeace left his office to do so. Spikings handed the phone to Dempsey, his hand still covering the mouthpiece.

'Oh it's for me is it?' asked Dempsey in mock surprise. Spikings wasn't playing. He thrust the phone into Dempsey's chest and removed his hand from the mouthpiece. Dempsey took it and put it to his ear.

'Hello?' He'd switched from his normal greeting because he didn't want to waste it on her.

'Jim?' It was her voice. He was pleased that he'd changed his greeting. He liked the fact that for once it was her who was asking the questions.

'Speaking,' he replied, as off-handedly as possible. Cathy recognized his voice now.

'Hey you got your black jacket on — looks real good.'

Dempsey glanced at his arm. *He* didn't even know which jacket he had on. But she was right. He *was* wearing his black jacket. Foley had hung it up for him when it had come back from the cleaners, or so he thought. But how did she know that he was wearing it, now? He twisted suddenly in order to look out the window of Spikings' office. The bottom half was frosted and through the top half Dempsey could only see trees. He realized that he was thinking irrationally. Just because she knew what he was wearing, there and then, didn't mean that she was watching him there and then. She could have seen him any-time. Though it was only 9:30 and all that he'd done that day was to get up and drive into the 'shop'. Makepeace re-entered. She saw at once that something had thrown Dempsey off balance.

Cathy, on the other end of the phone, also sensed that she'd thrown Dempsey off balance. She was in command again. She could do with him as she wanted.

'How are you anyway?' she continued as if talking to an old friend.

'Not as sick as you are,' retorted Dempsey. He was damned if he was going to talk to her as if *she* were an old friend.

Spikings and Makepeace looked at him trying to get him to cool down a bit. They needed time to trace the call and they didn't want Dempsey to anger her into putting the phone down. But there was no need to worry; Cathy only laughed at Dempsey's response.

'Only games,' she said, her tone one of reprimand.

'You got a real weird sense of humour,' Dempsey continued with the aggressive policy. But Cathy only laughed again. It was a mad laugh. It wasn't manic or cackling, it was just wrong. The laugh died down and she fell silent. Dempsey knew that he had to keep her talking but he didn't want to waste any of his chat-up lines on her. He searched for something else to say but his mind had gone blank, probably because on the other end of the line was the person he least wanted to have a telephone conversation with in the whole world.

Spikings came to his rescue. He held up an A4 sheet of paper on which he'd scribbled a large 'Y'. Dempsey got the message.

'Why are you doing this to me?' he asked.

'Out of ...' Cathy searched for the right word and found it 'love'.

'Well you got a real odd way of showing it.' The line fell silent again. Dempsey flicked through the pages of his memory, desperately trying to think of what he'd normally say in such situations.

'What's your name?' was all that he could come up with in the heat of the moment.

'Rumplestiltskin,' came back the answer almost before he had finished asking the question. He guessed that she'd heard that question before. But he didn't laugh at her riposte. He was in no mood for vaudeville.

'Who needs names?' she asked philosophically. But Dempsey was in no mood for philosophy either. All he wanted to do was to get this 'fruitcake' off the streets and out of his life as quickly as possible.

Spikings mouthed something at him which he didn't quite catch. Spikings mouthed it again but to Dempsey it just looked like an amateur goldfish impression. Spikings despaired.

'Meet,' he hissed at a level which he hoped would be audible to Dempsey but not to his femme fatale. Dempsey relayed the message.

'Er listen — why don't we meet?'

'Would you like that Jim?'

'Yeah I would like that very much,' replied Dempsey, not bothering to summon up very much enthusiasm. 'What d'you say? Where could we talk?'

'We're talking now,' she pointed out, obviously not impressed by his attempts at drawing her out into the open. She was enjoying listening to him struggling.

Makepeace looked up at him reassuringly. Dempsey was glad that he hadn't received this phone call alone in his flat.

'Yeah,' he continued 'but I mean, you know, person to person — you know that way we could look at each other — what d'you say?'

Cathy paused and looked around at the photographs of Dempsey on the wall. She noticed the one lying in tatters on the floor that she'd torn up the day before and was reminded of Makepeace's visit to Dempsey's apartment. She grew angry.

'You'll have to get rid of her,' she commanded. Dempsey was pretty sure who she meant by 'her' but he feigned innocence to give the boys in the tracing department more time to trace the call.

'Who?' he asked.

'Harry! You can't have both of us Jim.' Dempsey smiled across at Makepeace and shrugged his shoulders as if to apologize for being about to drop her.

'Oh Harry's nothing to me.' He said it casually, all the time watching Makepeace to witness her reactions. 'She's my chauffeur. She knows the streets, drives me around.'

Makepeace didn't enjoy her role in their partnership being described in such a way but, on the other hand, she was glad that Dempsey seemed to be enjoying the telephone conversation more, even if it was at her expense. Nonetheless she looked fierce, not wishing to disappoint him.

But Dempsey's running down of Makepeace's talents was wasted on Cathy. She didn't care what Makepeace's role was. If she were only Dempsey's shoe-shine boy she'd still want her dead.

'If she doesn't leave you alone, I'll kill her.'

'I thought you were gonna kill *me*,' he replied, attempting to draw her fire.

'I am.'

'Oh you're going to kill both of us huh? Well that's

an awful lot of killing.'

Cathy recognized the fact that Dempsey was waffling, trying to prolong the conversation. She decided to terminate it.

'Well ... time to go,' she said as if she had to go and take a cake out of the oven.

'No, no, no,' Dempsey desperately tried to milk some more time out of her. He didn't like the sudden reversal of roles. Now she was sounding calm and collected while he was madly trying to keep the lines open.

'Don't go — I'm enjoying this conversation — come on here — we've got a chance to talk — now I'm not busy you know — and er ...'

Cathy interrupted his procrastination with a contemptuous snort. She didn't like being taken for a gullible amateur.

'What, rap some more so as you can trace the number? Huh! I'm not that stupid Jim. Lots of love. I'll be watching you.'

'No, no, no, come on don't ...' but his protestations were too late. She'd already put the phone down. Dempsey put his phone down as well. He turned to Spikings. 'Long enough?' he asked without much confidence.

Spikings shook his head. 'Not a chance.'

Dempsey walked to the window and looked out. It was another lovely day, much like the day Barret had had his brains blown out on. He scanned the world outside to see if anyone was watching him there and then. The only living things he could see were the pigeons. He turned back to Spikings and Makepeace.

'How did she know what I was wearing?' he asked.

'Well she must have seen you.' Spikings felt that there was a certain security in stating the obvious.

'Yeah but when and where did she see me?'

'Well it must have been some place between here and your apartment.' Dempsey shook his head in disbelief, not at what Spikings had just said but that he should find himself in such a situation.

'This is really weird — it's almost as if I know who she is.'

'Just what I've always said,' Makepeace sounded a little smug. 'But the important thing is,' she continued, 'that we've found out that my being around obviously rubs salt into her wounds.'

'Well that's exactly what *I've* always said.' It was his turn to sound a little smug. But there was no time for him to rest on his laurels.

'So obviously I'm going to have to stay.' She said it as if she had just concluded some incontravertible piece of logical reasoning.

Dempsey didn't see it. 'How do you make that bright deduction, eh?'

'Put her out of her stride. She'll be so busy thinking about me that she'll trip up and make a mistake.'

Makepeace explained her plan calmly and collectedly. Dempsey wanted none of it. He felt that he could handle the whole thing himself and on top of that he really was afraid that she might get herself hurt.

'No!' he shouted, jumping to his feet and trying to stare her into submission. She looked across at Spikings for him to give his decision, the ruling decision. Dempsey looked at him also and it was obvious from the look which decision he favoured.

But Spikings was no master of physiognomy. He liked to weigh up everything purely objectively, discounting all emotional pressures. At least he liked to think he did so but, as Makepeace had experienced just before the phone call, he was really as prejudiced as the next man.

'Yes. She's got a point,' he said finally. 'We'll leave things as they are at present.'

Dempsey scowled at her, 'Who's the devious bastard now?'

'There's no need to swear Jim,' said Makepeace and swept out of the office, unable to surpress a broad grin of triumph.

Dempsey sat in Spikings' office for a moment longer. He was pleased that she was going to be with him but he wondered how he'd feel if she was killed. He'd lost a partner in New York once and though it wasn't his fault he'd almost quit the force. He always felt that *he'd* pull through difficult situations, as he didn't have the imagination to be able to think of *himself* dying, but if Harry were to. . . . It was too awful to think about. He thought about the fact that Makepeace had just called him Jim, instead. He wondered . . .

'Get on with some work,' yelled Spikings in his ear.

The rest of the day passed slowly. In the morning Dempsey reached what he thought was the half way point on his desk and they had a cup of coffee to celebrate. They also went out together to retrace Dempsey's journey from his apartment into the 'shop'. All they came up with was the sixty-year-old lollipop lady who was there every day. On closer inspection, however, she proved to be almost totally deaf and cross-eyed. She definitely wasn't their marksman. They drove home. It had been a pretty futile trip. There were thousands of windows lining the route of Dempsey's journey into work and there were thousands of people who he must pass unnoticed every day. Without anything more to go on than the fact that the killer was a five-foot-two woman, she was going to be difficult to trace.

* * *

In the afternoon they tried to chase up the rifle. It was standard MI5 issue but also available at most good hardware stores in America. They plumped for trying to squeeze something out of MI5, rather than out of half of Middle America. MI5 didn't let out any juice though. They, not surprisingly, refused to provide a list of all MI5 operatives who had been issued with such a rifle. They also refused to provide a list of all MI5 operatives who were psychologically unstable. Dempsey suggested that this might be because it would be rather a complete one. MI5 didn't get the joke. MI5 were concerned, of course, that there was a madwoman on the loose lessening London Transport's profit margins, but they didn't believe that it was really their problem. They suggested contacting hardware stores in Middle America.

Dempsey and Makepeace were both glad when the clock finally inched round to 5:30. Makepeace offered to come round to Dempsey's house to keep him company and perhaps to try and draw their attacker out into the open again. Dempsey offered to go round to her place to protect her in case the madwoman struck again. In the end they decided that they could both do with a bit of time apart. Dempsey wanted to go back and watch his favourite movie, which was being reshown on television, and Makepeace wanted to make sure that the decorators hadn't turned her drawing-room carpet into a Jackson Pollock or run off with the family silver. She insisted, however, on dropping round to Dempsey's place at about nine o'clock to give him her favourite plant, Henry, for safe keeping. She suspected that the decorators were slipping him the occasional tot of white spirit. They said goodbye in the car-park and went their separate ways.

Chapter
ELEVEN

On arriving home, Dempsey immediately went to the freezer compartment of the fridge and took out one of the TV dinners that he had bought a couple of days ago. He slipped off the cardboard sleeve and threw it into the kitchen rubbish bag. The sleeve bounced out so he bent down and pushed it to the bottom of the bag. In doing so he discovered the coffee-cup broken by Cathy. He picked it up and looked at it. It wasn't one of his favourite cups so he wasn't too upset. He assumed that it must have been Foley who'd done it during one of his 'security checks' that gave him a chance to snoop around everyone's apartments. He noticed that there were still two coffee-cups in the sink and smiled at Foley's attempt at deception. For a few seconds he toyed with the idea that the mad-woman might be Foley. He was in a position to see what Dempsey was wearing every morning. Perhaps he was like the Anthony Perkins figure in 'Psycho' with Mrs Foley rotting in a chair down in the boiler-room. The idea evaporated with the image of Foley putting on bright red lipstick and kissing photographs. He slid his supper into the microwave and pushed the button.

Three minutes later the microwave pinged and the door opened automatically. Dempsey wondered whether they'd produced a model that fed you as well. He took the silver-foil dish out of the microwave and removed the paper lid. It was hot, smelt alright and even bore a vague resemblance to real food. Dempsey hoped that it was also edible. He grabbed a beer from the fridge and settled himself in front of the television. This was the life he thought to himself. He grabbed hold of the remote control gadget on the table beside him and zapped the box into life. The familiar strains of the zither emerged from the set. *The Third Man* was just beginning. Dempsey sat back and relaxed to experience one of the few golden moments of the British cinema.

He'd seen the film scores of times before of course but every time he saw it, he tried to forget it as quickly as possible, so he could see it again as quickly as possible. The director's name came up on the screen, he was always amazed that it had been directed by a woman, and Dempsey stuck his fork into what he hoped was a piece of meat in order to get a mouthful in before the action proper started. But as he did so the television went on the blink. His first thought was that it something to do with his food, the spearing of the brown object and the buzzing of the television having happened so simultaneously. He rejected the idea. They put a lot of additives in food nowadays but not enough to do that. He sat back and waited for the subtitled apology from the television company, but it was not forthcoming. In the end he was forced to admit that there was something wrong with his own set. This hadn't been his day. In fact these last three days hadn't been his days.

He removed his supper from his lap and struggled out of his armchair, hoping that giving the television a hearty thump would cure it of its buzzing and him of his frustrations. But just before his fist made contact, the sound returned, as clear as a bell. He thumped the set regardless but fortunately didn't affect the sound. He sighed resignedly and moved back towards his armchair. As he did so the buzzing started up again. It was as if someone up there was toying with him. As flies to wanton boys are we to the BBC, he thought to himself wryly. He walked back towards the television set and inevitably the sound returned. He went to sit down and it started again. He thought to himself how easily amused the Gods were.

He prowled round the set threateningly, not really knowing what he was looking for but perhaps hoping to find a gremlin that he could decapitate. Unfortunately there wasn't one. He did find, however, that the interference disappeared only when he stood in a certain position, the position he had stood in when thumping the television. Dempsey tried standing there. Joseph Cotton had just met Trevor Howard but Dempsey was unable to concentrate on what they were saying as he was developing a crick in his back. Though the film had been shot with the camera at strange angles, Dempsey was sure that Carol Reed hadn't intended it to be watched at strange angles. Dempsey was reminded of the days when his family had had a television with a home-made indoor aerial. Sometimes they'd had to Sellotape it to the ceiling to get anything that was even remotely watchable and other times they had got perfect reception from television channels four states away.

This was an external aerial though, and the set had never played up before. Dempsey was puzzled. By trial and error he found out that the sound was at its very best when he stood directly between the television and his reading light. The distance between him and the television didn't matter but if he strayed either side of this line the buzzing started up almost immediately. He was pleased with this domestic detective work. His conclusion was that there must be a loose connection in his reading light. He picked it up and examined it. Suddenly he dropped it, he'd burnt his fingers on the bulb. He switched it off. He pulled the flex and shook it. There didn't really seem much that could go wrong with it. He turned it upside down to examine the base and as he did so he froze as if he were playing musical statues. The interference on the television grew worse. Joseph Cotton sounded like a dalek.

But Dempsey wasn't listening to him. He was staring in horror at what he'd found stuck inside the base of his reading lamp. It was a bugging device. He placed the lamp back on the table as gently as if it had been a bomb. He had no doubts about who had planted it and it sickened him to think of his private life being invaded in such a way. Still he hoped that she hadn't heard him pick up the lamp or even if she had, he hoped she didn't think that he'd discovered the bug. For as the feeling of nausea wore off an idea took its place.

Dempsey needn't have worried. Cathy had been listening in but immediately on hearing the television being turned on she'd switched her receiver off. At present she was writing Dempsey a love poem. She'd written him love poems before, in fact she had a drawer full of them but she hadn't got around to sending any of them off as yet. She thought that she might read one of them at his funeral.

Dempsey left the television on and crept as quietly as possible out of his living room, down the hall and out of his apartment, closing the door behind him. He had an urgent phone call to make. He tiptoed towards the stairs glancing back at his apartment as if the bugs were about to crawl out of the woodwork and follow him. All clear, he turned swiftly and bumped right into Foley who was waiting by the lift, probably for the same carpet that Dempsey had attacked down in the laundry. Dempsey jumped back a foot at this unexpected contact. Foley looked at him as if he were mad. Dempsey apologized and Foley was understanding, if a little humouring. Dempsey continued down the stairs and Foley continued waiting for the life. But a couple of steps down the stairs Dempsey stopped. The discovery of the bug had set his mind racing and the collision with Foley had re-introduced another question. He walked thoughtfully back up the stairs to Foley.

'Mr Foley?'

His sudden re-appearance startled the old man but he was quick to recover himself. He knew that Dempsey was mad but he didn't think that he was dangerous. 'Yeah.'

'My black jacket came back from the cleaners.'

'Yeah.'

'When?'

Foley rubbed a stubberly chin in thought. 'Er, Tuesday.'

'You sure?'

'Sure.' He nodded but then became concerned at Dempsey's apparent concern. 'I mean I didn't . . .'

'No, no, no, no it was fine, it was fine.' Dempsey thought as he spoke, He couldn't think what had happened on Tuesday and he still assumed that it was Foley who had hung up his jacket in his wardrobe. He decided that he'd try and work out about the jacket later, the most important thing at the moment was to tell Spikings and the boys in electronics about the bugs. He started off down the stairs again but as he did so he caught Foley's pitiful expression. Poor Foley obviously thought that Dempsey thought he'd done something wrong with the jacket. Dempsey tried to explain to him.

'I just needed to know *when*, that's all. Thanks very much.'

Dempsey descended the stairs once again leaving Foley looking much relieved. He didn't want to be accused of doing anything unfairly.

'Goodnight,' he shouted after him. But he still wondered why Dempsey was so concerned about what day he'd returned the jacket. Perhaps the cleaners hadn't done a good job. But the girl . . . he suddenly remembered the girl with no clothes on. Perhaps he'd been wrong to give the jacket to her. Perhaps she'd done something to it. He didn't want to be blamed for that. He yelled down the stairwell to Dempsey.

'I gave it to the young lady.'

Dempsey stopped in his tracks. 'Young lady?' He ran up the stairs towards Foley again. Foley heard the footsteps and felt that he should have kept his trap shut. Dempsey arrived back on his level panting. The question still echoed in the stairwell.

'Yes,' answered Foley warily.

Dempsey tried to get things straight. Foley was sometimes a little confused and sometimes a little confusing.

'There was a lady ... in my apartment?' he asked.

Foley couldn't work out why Dempsey was sounding so surprised. He didn't feel that he was a nosey man but he couldn't have help noticing ladies going in and out of Dempsey's apartment.

'Yes she let me in.' No that was wrong. That was imagination not memory. He corrected himself. 'Well she opened the door.'

'Can you describe her?' Dempsey sounded eager. He sensed a break.

'Well.' Foley closed his eyes in thought for a moment. 'She didn't have any clothes on.'

'You mean she was in the buff?' prompted Dempsey.

Foley shook his head, he wasn't going to be tricked into giving false evidence. 'Oh I couldn't say whether she was in the bath or not. But err. ...'

Dempsey interrupted. 'No, no, buff, naked.' At another time Dempsey would have found Foley's miscomprehension amusing but at present matters were too pressing.

'Oh I see ... well she was naked underneath your robe, yes.' Foley wondered whether Dempsey was perhaps testing his powers of observation. So he was surprised to see that Dempsey seemed to be severely affected by this news. Suddenly he twigged. 'You mean you weren't there?'

Dempsey looked up at him worriedly. 'Not only was I not there, I didn't know she was!' Dempsey climbed down the stairs thoughtfully. 'Goodnight, Mr Foley.'

'Goodnight.'

The boys from electronics were having the time of their lives. Bugging, or more accurately de-bugging, was one of their favourite jobs. For it they had a special little black box with an aerial and a red light that flashed faster and faster the nearer to the bug that it was placed. There were three of them and they took it in turns to work the machine. They looked as if they were flying invisible radio-controlled aeroplanes. They also kept totally quiet which gave them the air of stalking some easily scared animal. There was no real need to be creeping around the house as they also had another little black box with a light that could tell them whether the bugs were being listened into at the time. At present the light wasn't on which meant that no one was listening in. The boys from electronics kept acting as if there was someone listening though, as it made the game much more fun.

Arthur Wilson was also there with another of the boys from forensics. They were taking fingerprints. Most of them were Dempsey's but there were two sets of prints from smaller hands, women's hands.

Dempsey watched them all go about their business. He wasn't enjoying having grown men playing games in his apartment but he knew that it might provide a lead. He didn't hold out great hopes for the fingerprints as only a small percentage of the population have their prints on file. The presence of the bugs, however, had given him an idea. He watched as Arthur Wilson dusted down his gym equipment for prints. He seemed to be sprinkling graphite powder all over the place. He couldn't bear to watch his recently cleaned apartment being turned into the inside of a pencil box. He decided to go somewhere quiet to try and think of something else.

Watson was there also. He was supervising the arrangments as Dempsey was technically not allowed to, being off duty. He was watching over the locksmith, who was changing the locks, when Makepeace arrived carrying Henry, her plant. She was surprised to see Watson outside the front door of Dempsey's apartment, on his hands and knees apparently looking through his keyhole. She was about to make some witty remark when Watson stopped her speaking with a raised hand.

'Whisper,' he whispered.

Makepeace smiled. It was a bit like a party game. 'Hello Watson. What's going on?'

'Bugs.'

Makepeace looked puzzled. 'What kind of bugs?'

'Electronic ones. What kind do you think? Pest control doesn't do emergency calls at nine o'clock in the evening.'

Makepeace handed Watson her plant. 'Well make sure that this doesn't get any bugs.' She brushed past him leaving him looking as if he were left holding a baby rather than a miniature hybrid hydrangea. She turned before she entered. 'Where's Dempsey?' she whispered.

'He's in the bathroom, I think.'

Makepeace looked concerned and Watson explained.

'It's less busy in there.'

Makepeace glanced into the living room before making her way down the hall to the bathroom. The electronics boys had just unearthed a second bug in there and were clustered around it as happy as if they had just won the pools. She pushed the bathroom door tentatively open to reveal Dempsey sitting on the

171

edge of the bath looking disconsolate.

'Can we talk?' she mouthed.

Dempsey beckoned her in. She shut the door gently behind her and sat down next to him.

'Fire away,' he said with mock eagerness.

'What's going on?'

'I've had a lady visitor.'

'In here?' Makepeace looked around the cramped confines of the bathroom in amazement.

'Here, there, everywhere. She's bugged everywhere as well.'

Things began to fall in place for Makepeace, just as they had done for Dempsey when he had first discovered the bug.

'Ah, so that's how she knows so much about you,' she exclaimed. Dempsey nodded. 'I wonder how much she does know. How long those bloody things have been in here.'

Makepeace swallowed. It was an unpleasant thought. She wondered how she'd feel if she found out that someone had been listening in to everything that she said and did. She reckoned she'd feel terrible. She could sympathize with Dempsey but she couldn't think of anything that she could say to make him feel better. She let her gaze wander around the white enamel of the bathroom. In doing so she noticed a small black handprint on the side of the bath, it looked as if a sweep had been in there. In fact it was where graphite powder had been used to show up a set of fingerprints.

'Those her prints?' asked Makepeace.

'Dempsey shrugged. 'Could be.'

'It's a woman's hand.'

'Well she's been in here ... prowling around ... wearing my robe ...'

Makepeace suddenly remembered where she had smelt that perfume before. It had been for a fleeting instant while she had been changing into her work-out clothes in Dempsey's bedroom.

'I thought I smelt perfume the other day.' She said it as much to remind herself as to inform Dempsey. But she still didn't feel that the memory was complete.

'She even answered the door.' Dempsey continued listing her misdemeanours.

'It's almost as if she wants to be caught.'

'Well I reckon that we ought to oblige her then.' Makepeace nodded her head wisely. 'Easier said than done.'

'Oh I don't know. I'm sure if we put our heads together we could concoct a little something.'

Dempsey was getting at something but Makepeace wasn't sure what, though, judging by the broadness of his grin, she felt sure that she wasn't going to like it.

At that moment Watson entered. He made the OK sign, gave Dempsey his new set of keys and left. Dempsey and Makepeace went back into the living-room. Everything looked much the same as it had done before the invasion, apart from the fact that there was a red sticker on his reading light to indicate that it contained a bug, and another one on the top of the bookcase, where they'd discovered a second. Watson had left the device that indicated whether the bugs were receiving or not. The light wasn't on. Watson had also got the boys from electronics to install a small speaker that emitted a beep when the receiver was switched on, so as Dempsey wouldn't go mad watching the red light all the time.

At present, however, both of them were too tired to say anything that they didn't want anyone else to

173

hear. Makepeace gave Dempsey some brief instructions about looking after her plant but he didn't take them in, though he remembered that they involved something to do with water. She promised to collect it as soon as the decorators had finished their work, said goodnight and left.

Dempsey slumped down in his armchair. He looked across at his TV dinner. It looked back at him coldly. It threatened food-poisoning so he ignored the encouragements of his stomach. He couldn't even watch television. He went to the fridge, grabbed another can of beer and picked up the nearest book. It was, of course, Edgar Allen Poe. He threw it onto the floor and plumped for the early night. In the bedroom there was a red sticker on his bed board. He looked at it and hoped that he snored loudly.

Chapter
TWELVE

Dempsey and Makepeace met in the SI 10 carpark the following morning at nine precisely. They both lied about how well they'd slept again.

The morning passed inexorably slowly. Although they now had lots of evidence about the woman's past movements, they still didn't know who she was. Foley had been able to tell them nothing about her other than that she was naked, had dark fair hair and was about five-foot-six; his measurements of height all being based on the yardstick of his own desire to think himself much taller. So all they could do was to sit and wait for the report on the fingerprints from Dempsey's apartment. The chance that the woman's prints were on file was small if they were lucky.

But an awaited fingerprint report never comes, or so it seems to the waiters. Makepeace tried to pass the time by telling Dempsey about the new colour scheme that she'd planned for her house. Dempsey tried to appear interested but his powers of deception weren't developed enough to deceive Makepeace and so she dropped it and went over to talk to Johnson and Matthey about the recent developments in their case. Dempsey reverted to tidying his desk but even that task wasn't Herculean enough to outlast the compilation of the fingerprint report. He took to tapping his biro on the desk in time with the second hand of the clock. He tried to speed up his tapping to see if that would speed up the passage of time. It seemed to slow it down. Makepeace returned with two more cups of coffee. He tried to relate the plot of *The Third Man* to her, as she said that she'd never seen it. But unfortunately he'd forgotten it too well. All that he could remember was the cat, Orson Welles and a bit of the speech about the cuckoo clock. From Makepeace's bemused expression, he realized that he wasn't really doing the film justice so he resorted to telling Makepeace not to miss it next time that it was on television.

Eventually, after enough cups of coffee to waken the dead, Watson entered, clasping the report. His face and voice were deadpan.

'Here are the dabs from your place.'

'Any luck?' asked Dempsey.

'Luck doesn't come into it,' replied Watson, obviously enjoying keeping them on tenterhooks.

Dempsey felt that he'd waited quite long enough, but he'd got so far without blowing his cool that he was determined he wouldn't let Watson rile him now.

'How about success then?'

'Success.' Watson thought for a moment. 'Yes.' Watson grinned and Dempsey and Makepeace looked mightily relieved.

'What's her name then?' asked Dempsey eagerly.

Watson opened the folder and ran his finger down the page.

'The set of prints in the bathroom were those of a ...' he paused and looked up, 'Miss Harriet Makepeace.' He smirked.

Dempsey moved in for the kill. Watson realized that his comic timing was wrong and prevented him with an upheld hand and a loud:

'But ...'

Dempsey paused waiting to see if Watson could think up some good last words. Watson loosened his collar and continued anxiously.

'... we did find a large number of another set of prints ...'

'They better not turn out to be mine,' interrupted Dempsey fiercely.

'No, they belong to a ...' Watson checked hurriedly through the folder, 'a Warren, Catherine Warren.'

Dempsey switched from the offensive into the pensive. He'd expected the mention of the name to strike him like a thunderbolt but this wasn't even a shock from a nylon carpet. He shook his head.

'Never heard of her, any aliases?'

Watson looked through the folder once more.

'No, none known ... used to work for MI5 though.'

'Well that explains some of her expertise,' added Makepeace, glad to have at least one piece of the jig-saw.

'Yeah,' went on Watson, 'apparently she went a little bit ... er you know — it's all in the folder.'

'And that explains the inexplicability of her behaviour.' Makepeace sounded angry, but it wasn't with Watson, it was with MI5. They could have told

177

them about her when they'd first made enquiries about the rifle.

Watson closed the folder and handed it to Dempsey who was still trying to rack his brains to remember if he'd ever come across a Catherine Warren. He couldn't even think of a Catherine that he'd ever known well.

He opened the file and the thunderbolt struck. There, clipped to the inside of the folder, was a photograph of Cathy, the waitress in his favourite, or rather ex-favourite, hamburger joint. Seeing his reaction, Makepeace looked over his shoulder to see the contents of the folder. She recognized Cathy also. Yet another piece of the jig-saw fell into place; that other time that she'd smelt that perfume. It had been when Cathy had bent over her to reposition the flowers. She remembered thinking at the time that there had been something strange about the spilling of the water, but it was all too easy to be wise after the event. She looked across at Dempsey. He was still staring at the photograph. Things were coming back to him also. It now seemed so obvious to him that the voice on the phone had been an American voice, her voice, in fact. As he remembered her it suddenly seemed that she had always behaved strangely. He also remembered the tipping of the water over Makepeace. But even so, water-tipping was a far cry from murder.

Dempsey walked into 'Nathan Detroit's' with Makepeace beside him. The place wasn't yet open, even though the door was, and no one appeared to be there, not even Catherine Warren.

Paula, the waitress who had handed Dempsey his

paper last time that he was in there, appeared from behind the bar. She spoke to them across the room.

'You're too keen. We're not open yet.'

Dempsey and Makepeace walked up to the bar to talk to her.

'I know that,' said Dempsey. 'I'm looking for Cathy. Is she here? It's important.'

'She's gone. Quit.'

'When?'

Paula was surprised at the urgency of Dempsey's question. 'Two evenings ago.' She picked up a cloth and began to wipe down the bar thoughtfully.

'In fact it was just after she spilt water over your friend here.' She gestured towards Makepeace. The gesture contained an element of contempt. Makepeace wasn't sure why, but she smiled back sweetly regardless.

'You got her home address?' asked Dempsey.

Paula shook her head. 'Boss might though.'

'Great, where could I find him?'

'He's away,' she answered surlily. Paula was in no mood for being helpful. Dempsey was surprised. She was normally very friendly towards him. He thought for a moment that she might be in league with Cathy. But it was a dumb thought; lunatics very seldom had accomplices and if they did they looked like Ygor, not like Paula.

'Where could we find him?' asked Makepeace.

'I don't know. He often just disappears and won't tell anyone where he's gone or where he's been when he comes back.'

'Well when do you expect him back?' continued Makepeace.

Paula shrugged. 'I don't know ... a few days?'

Makepeace, who didn't even know how friendly

Paula was normally, was also surprised by her reluctance to be of help.

Dempsey took over. He didn't care how much Paula objected to being questioned; she knew Cathy better than they did and it was important that they learned as much about Cathy from her as possible.

'It's a bit sudden isn't it? Her leaving like that.'

'Yeah, out of the blue.' She stopped wiping the bar for a moment. 'She didn't mention it to you?'

'No.'

Paula looked surprised at first and then disbelieving.

Dempsey realized that Paula was harbouring some kind of misconception.

'Why d'you think she might have?' he asked.

Paula's look of disbelief turned back to one of surprise. 'Well I knew that you two were close — especially after her birthday.'

'Her birthday?' echoed Dempsey blankly.

Paula thought that he was kidding her at first but looking into his eyes she realized that he wasn't. 'You know.' She insisted.

'Remind me,' insisted Dempsey in turn.

She laughed at the suggestion that Dempsey might need to be reminded but Dempsey looked so serious she decided that she had better play along.

'Well she never stopped talking about it. She brought the roses in here you know. Kept them on the bar. There's still one tucked behind the cash register — a dead one.'

'She told you that I bought her roses?'

'Yes,' replied Paula sharply, misinterpreting Dempsey's question and thinking that he was indignant about Cathy telling her about the gift, rather than about Cathy telling a lie. Dempsey turned to Makepeace.

'We got a real lulu here, Harry.'

But Makepeace knew Dempsey and she wasn't so sure that he was as uninvolved with the girl as he was trying to make out. 'Did you take her out that night?' she asked.

'Yeah.' He recognized her suspicions and was immediately on the defensive. 'But I took her for a quick drink and that's all.'

'Where?' persisted Makepeace.

'A cocktail bar, two blocks from here.'

'How long did that last?'

'Ten minutes max.' Dempsey stared into Makepeace's eyes, trying to impress upon her the truth of what he was saying.

Paula had given up all pretence of wiping the bar by now and was watching Makepeace firing off questions at Dempsey, thinking that she was witnessing a married partner's quarrel about Dempsey's infidelity with Cathy. She couldn't just stand by and listen to one of her friends and colleagues being called a liar. Cathy really was in love with Dempsey. She knew that. And, though it was really none of her business and she didn't want to be responsible for breaking up what might have remained a happy marriage, she felt that she owed it to Cathy, and perhaps even to the two of them to make sure that the truth came out.

'If that's so,' she butted in, 'then how come the pianist was playing her favourite tune as you walked in? You saying that you didn't fix that?' She leant back, amused at the predicament she thought she'd put Dempsey in.

Dempsey twisted round to face her. 'You ever been there?' he asked sharply.

'On my wages?!'

'There is no pianist,' he said with finality.

For a moment Paula was taken aback by this but she soon recovered her voice. 'Well that's easy to say isn't it.' Dempsey seemed to believe this so earnestly that she began to suspect that he was mad.

Dempsey thought she was being pig-headed and he had no time for it. He reached forward over the counter to grab hold of her arm. 'Alright I'll take you there then.'

Paula shook her arm free. 'Drop dead. I wouldn't go anywhere with a fruitcake like you.'

Dempsey tried to remain calm. 'What makes you think that *I'm* the fruitcake?'

'Well I know for a fact that you've been going out with Cathy ever since you started coming in here. You used to meet secretly. She's told me everything about you.'

'Oh yeah, what's she told you about me?' he asked agressively.

But Paula was not going to be threatened. She had the safety of the bar between her and Dempsey and she had Makepeace as a witness for anything he might do.

'Oh everything, believe me,' she said suggestively. 'She's told me about your car, what your apartment's like. She tells me everything that you say to her and everything that you do together.'

'Has she told you what I do?' asked Dempsey, his voice calm and measured in strong contrast to Paula's loud claims.

'What do you mean, what you do?'

'What I do for a living?'

'Yes, of course she's told me that,' she said indignantly.

'And what did she say that I did?' continued

Dempsey as if trying to talk a two-year-old into handing over a fragile object.

'You're a commodity broker.'

At that Dempsey reached into his pocket and produced his badge. He thrust it into her face.

'You've been taken for a ride sweetheart, she's the one who's the fruitcake.'

The colour suddenly left Paula's cheek. She looked as if she'd just been told of the death of a close friend. In a way she had. Someone who she had thought that she knew quite well had turned out to be someone completely different. The firm ground of truth had suddenly pulled from beneath her feet. For a while she didn't know what to believe. All that she did know was that she felt physically sick. She rushed out to the back of the restaurant.

Dempsey watched her go. He hadn't meant to break the truth to her as bluntly as he had done. He knew that it would be a difficult thing for her to handle because a similar thing had just happened to him with the same person and *he* hardly knew Cathy at all whereas Paula obviously knew her quite well.

'She'll be all right,' reassured Makepeace, reading his expression.

'She's not on the hit list at least.' Dempsey tried to reassure himself.

Makepeace corrected him. 'She's not in the gold and silver medal positions at least.'

Dempsey looked around the restaurant that had gone so far towards making up for the disappointments of his basketball team. He doubted if he'd ever be able to visit the place again, however things turned out.

'We've got to get her before she kills anyone else,' said Dempsey as if trying to steel himself for the task ahead.

'We've got to get her before she kills *us*,' corrected Makepeace. 'And I've had an idea that I think might help.'

Dempsey wasn't in the mood to feed back the required question. He just waited for Makepeace to fill him in.

'What if she could see you as well as hear you?'

Dempsey thought about the question. The answer was that she would be much easier to catch and the probability that Makepeace was right seemed to be quite high. In fact the more he thought about it the more likely it seemed. It was standard SI 10 procedure to combine visual and aural surveillance. It was probably MI 5 policy as well. They decided to wait until the evening to put their theory to the test.

Chapter
THIRTEEN

When they got back to the office they put the finishing touches to their plan. It wasn't, however, very complicated so it didn't take them long. Neither Dempsey nor Makepeace told Spikings about their plan as they knew that he wouldn't like it and would try and put a stop to it. Spikings' approach to the problem would have been to send out squads to search every house within a square mile of Dempsey's apartment. Neither of them wanted that; it would be slow and might well drive their quarry underground. Dempsey and Makepeace wanted the job done quickly and they wanted to do it themselves.

Both of them left work early, giving Spikings different excuses, and met up again in Dempsey's apartment. Dempsey scanned the windows of the mansion block opposite through his binoculars. He stood back from the window in the hope that he wouldn't be spotted himself.

'Anything?' asked Makepeace, standing at his shoulder.

Dempsey scanned across the windows. 'Well ... there's a woman watering her window box ...' he scanned along one floor and then down to the next. '... a boy playing the violin ... a naked man working out with weights.'

Makepeace leant forward eagerly trying to catch a glimpse with her naked eye. 'Where?'

Dempsey handed her the binoculars and pointed in the right direction. Makepeace looked through them.

'I don't see anything.'

'Third floor second from the left,' directed Dempsey.

Makepeace caught sight of him 'Oh yes ...' Then got a good look at him, '... oh my god, he looks like a walrus.'

'Serves you right for being such a peeping tom,' reprimanded Dempsey. Makepeace ignored him and continued with the search.

'Good grief what time is it?' she asked, still looking through the binoculars and obviously amazed by something she'd just seen.

Dempsey looked at his watch. 'About five-thirty.' He was intrigued to find out what Makepeace had seen.

'My God they start early,' she smirked.

'Who start early?' asked Dempsey his curiosity now really roused.

Makepeace handed him the binoculars. 'Fourth floor, middle window.'

'Dempsey took the binoculars eagerly and focused on the fourth floor middle window. But to his disappointment all that he could see was a family seated round their kitchen table having a meal. He rested the binoculars on his knee and looked across at Makepeace accusingly.

'Serves you right for having such a dirty mind.' She laughed.

They decided to call a halt to their search. They had gambled that Cathy knew so much about Dempsey's habits that she wouldn't be watching before five-thirty as she knew that Dempsey wasn't normally back from work until then. They'd hoped that they might have been able to see a bugging device on a table or a rifle leant against a wall but they hadn't. Now it had reached five-thirty they felt that searching would be too dangerous. She would see them looking long before they saw her looking, as she knew which window they'd appear at, whereas she could appear at any one of hundreds. They hung up the binoculars and sat down to watch the little black box.

'Coffee?' offered Dempsey. They seemed to have spent the whole of the last four days waiting and drinking coffee, apart from when someone was trying to murder them that is.

'Please. I don't want to fall asleep.'

Dempsey smiled. The plan was to wait until Watson's black box beeped and then to proceed to make love, or rather, to make the noises of making love. Dempsey had suggested that if they were going to be professional about it they should *really* make love, as Cathy would be bound to spot the difference. But Makepeace insisted that she was a very good actress. The theory behind their love-making was that listening to it would sufficiently rile Cathy into showing her hand and revealing her position. It was a dangerous plan. She might decide to show her hand by taking pot shots at them or hurling a bomb through the window, but these were dangers that they were prepared to face if it gave them a chance of getting her off the streets.

Dempsey entered with the coffees and handed Makepeace hers. They sat down on the sofa in silence and stared blankly at Watson's box. They both felt nervous, like kids on their first date. It wasn't the love-making that they were worried about, it was what might follow it. They weren't worried about getting pregnant but about getting killed. If they'd had time they would have erected a large sheet of bullet-proof glass in front of the window. Then, if they were shot at, they would be safe and they could easily work out, by aligning the hole made in the window and the mark made by the bullet on the bullet-proof glass, which window the bullet came from. But they hadn't had time for any of this so they were just hoping that she didn't try and settle her problems with little bits of lead or that, if she did, she was off target, as she had been at the bus stop. They stared at the box willing it to stay silent.

'What if it doesn't go off?' asked Makepeace, betraying her thoughts.

'Then I guess that you and I are going to sit here and grow old together.'

Makepeace glanced across at him. He looked as if he was rather looking forwrd to the prospect. Makepeace looked down at her coffee again. It was instant and bitter but preferable to the sight of Dempsey looking cheerful. She idly tried to rub her lipstick off the rim of the cup. She wished that she was at home tearing a strip off the decorators but her main wish was that Catherine Warren was out of her life. The seconds seemed stuck in treacle. She recapped in her mind the events that had brought her to that particular sofa on that particular evening waiting to have her brains blown out for she didn't particularly know what reason. The chief thing that had brought her there was the fact that Dempsey's favourite movie was *The Third Man*. If it had been *Play Misty For Me* on the television he probably would have turned the set off and not bothered to find out what was interfering with it. It was also luck that the bug had started interfering at all. She said as much to Dempsey.

'It wasn't luck,' he replied slightly scornfully. 'It was faulty wiring inside that bug.'

'Well it was very lucky that the bug was faultily wired, then,' persisted Makepeace.

But Dempsey didn't seem willing to accept the fact that, if it weren't for one inadequate bit of soldering, they might have had another couple of days of the hell that they were experiencing at the moment.

'It was an error that's all. All police work is based on error. A crime without errors is a perfect crime and therefore whoever committed the crime is untraceable.'

Makepeace didn't bother to argue. She still thought they had been lucky. Though sitting on the sofa willing Catherine Warren to die of natural causes before she could switch on the bugging device, it seemed like an odd kind of luck.

Two more minutes passed in silence. Dempsey got up and began to pace around to relieve the tension. He went to the window and looked out. The walrus had finished working out and was now eating greedily in another window. The family had washed up and were watching television. It looked like any other late spring afternoon, though it was probably more beautiful than most. Everyone seemed to be minding their own business. But out there there was also someone who was minding his and Makepeace's business, minding it so much in fact that she wanted to kill them. He walked away from the window.

'Fancy a little romantic music to put us in the mood?' he asked casually.

'No thanks. I think that it might interfere with the sound reception.'

'OK. So long as you think that you can handle it without additional stimulants.'

'What do you mean handle it?' objected Make-peace.

'Handle playing a love scene with me. I mean you haven't had much experience. . . .'

'I've had quite enough experience to keep up with your clichéd patter, thanks very much,' interrupted Makepeace.

Dempsey was pleased that he'd ruffled her feathers. He was, in a way, rather looking forward to their love scene and in a way, so was she.

'I think that you might be pleasantly surprised . . .' began Dempsey but was interrupted. The box had bleeped. They looked at each other as if they hadn't believed that it would really ever happen. Dempsey suddenly realized that, listening the other end, Cathy might have heard his sentence trailing off. He tried to make it sound as if it were a dramatic pause.

'. . . by the new me.' His voice had become suave and husky. Makepeace was tempted to laugh but didn't. Dempsey walked away from the window to the edge of the sofa on which she was sitting. He decided to start again and play it open and honest.

'Sure I er ran around a lot, but that was before, er because.' He faltered momentarily. People trying to express their love are often tongue tied. Dempsey

190

hoped that Cathy would interpret it that was anyhow. 'But er I've changed — I mean with you it's different.'

'I wonder how many times you've said that before?' Makepeace asked with a note of cynicism that Dempsey didn't think was entirely appropriate for the scene that they were supposed to be playing. She stood up and moved to the other end of the sofa away from Dempsey. He didn't think that the movement was entirely appropriate either. But now it was his turn.

'No. What I feel about you, Harry, is special, very special.' He tried to sound as sincere as possible.

The two of them were now standing at opposite ends of the sofa. To anyone watching it would have seemed a very odd love scene. But no one was watching. They weren't visible through the window and so Cathy was merely listening in on the bugging device and she didn't think that there was anything strange about their conversation. She really believed that Dempsey was clumsily trying to declare his love for Makepeace and it made her mad. She had sensed that Dempsey had been lying to her earlier, on the phone, when he had said that Makepeace was no more than his chauffeur. Now she knew that this was true. Tears welled up in her eyes. She believed that Dempsey had been her lover and was now being unfaithful to her with Makepeace.

Makepeace herself was less taken in by Dempsey's performance. She waited for more of the same but Dempsey's gesture to her told her that it was now her turn. She knew that she had to reply quickly or it would sound suspicious but all that she could come up with at such short notice was:

'I didn't realize.'

Dempsey looked despairing at her lack of imagination but there was no time for recrimination. The ball was now in his court and he had to keep it rolling.

'Oh well why should you?' he said off-handedly. 'I mean we spend every waking moment together — it's er, it's a wonder that we're not bored to tears. . . .'

He ran out of steam and motioned to Makepeace for some help. She really was looking bored to tears by the whole thing but realizing that Dempsey was in a bit of difficulty said the first thing that came into her head.

'I'm not bored to tears.'

Dempsey raised his eyes to the heavens in despair. He didn't feel that she was pulling her weight. He decided to return the hospital pass.

'Are you sure?' he asked his voice tinged with an aggression that he hoped Cathy wouldn't notice. It was a question that he thought would force Makepeace into a long speech.

'Yes,' she answered sweetly.

Dempsey became exasperated. It was his fault, he supposed, for asking a question that could be answered with a 'yes' or a 'no' but it was as if Makepeace refused to believe that he was acting and was trying to fend off a real declaration of love. This wasn't the way that they were going to draw Cathy out into the open. An admission of not being bored to tears by someone's presence wasn't exactly what Dempsey had had in mind when he had mentioned the idea of the love scene and he doubted that it was the kind of thing that would make Cathy blow her top and show her hand. He tried to communicate to Makepeace how unhelpful she was being without giving the game away to their listener.

'I don't wanna have to put words in your mouth,' he said ambiguously. He tried to reinforce the message with a bit of telepathy.

Makepeace got the message but then became tongue tied. She opened her mouth but no words came out. Having fought off Dempsey's advances and joke-advances for so long it was difficult to suddenly turn around and surrender herself to them and to him. It was even more difficult to start making them herself. She opened her mouth again but still nothing came out. Dempsey appreciated the effort but not the result. He stepped in again to fend off the silence.

'At first I thought ... er ... that this was just an affair but I realize now that it is much more.' Despite the seriousness of the situation he was unable to suppress a smile as he heard himself cooing such meaningless clichées with such sincerity. He desperately fought against trying to let any hint of this amusement show in his voice.

But he needn't have worried. Cathy was no longer paying any attention to the length of pauses in their conversation or to exactness of tone. Things had gone beyond that. All she knew now was that her lover was trying to make love to another. She glanced across at the photographs of Dempsey on her wall as if she had seen them move. Dempsey stared back at her. He was smiling. He was taunting her, torturing her. She picked up an ashtray and hurled it against the wall.

Makepeace untied her tongue and shook off her stage fright. Dempsey's smile had reminded her that it really was only a game and she became determined to give as good as she got.

'What are you saying?' she asked proudly. 'Do you think that you can love *me*?' She said 'me' as if she were Mata Hari herself. Dempsey grinned. He'd never heard her speak like that before. He rather liked it. He moved in her direction but she held up her hand to prevent him. 'I don't mean now,' she back tracked fearing, from the look on Dempsey's face, she had rather overplayed her *femme fatale* role. 'I mean in the weeks and months to come.'

At the mention of the idea of the long term relationship Dempsey walked back to his end of the sofa again. Mata Hari had submerged below for the present.

'Love's not a word I use easily,' responded Dempsey. The line reminded him of nights spent at the drive-in movies.

'Me neither.'

'Although I wake up in the morning and my first thought is of you. ...' He looked Makepeace up and down suggestively. It was the kind of look that wouldn't come across on short wave radio.

Makepeace realized that, when Dempsey talked about waking up in the morning, he was suggesting the ideas of nudity and bed, but she willfully twisted his phrase round to something far less suggestive.

'It's the same for me. I sit there in the kitchen in the morning with my tea and toast and, in a funny sort of way, I actually look forward to going to work with you. ...'

Dempsey sneered at her. The last time that tea and toast had got anyone aroused was the Boston Tea Party.

But Catherine Warren was mad and getting madder all the time. She didn't care that looking forward to going to work with someone in a funny sort of way wasn't a particularly romantic thing to say. All her objective faculties were swamped by her burning hatred of the two of them. Their voices filled her flat, declaring love for one another. She didn't care what language they couched it in, she just knew, with a certainty that only the mad can achieve, that the two of them were really in love. The photographs of Dempsey were laughing now. Laughing at her because she'd never known love, never known true love and now at her age probably never would. She grabbed a knife out of her chest of drawers and stabbed at the photographs of Dempsey. She'd stop him laughing.

Dempsey was not amused by Makepeace's deliberate dampening attempt. He stood there waiting for her to wax passionate again but she much preferred their conversation when it was on a domestic rather than a passionate level and was determined to keep at that level. Dempsey, on the other hand, was determined to shake her out of this mood. His voice became harsh and forceful.

'I wanna hold your hand. I wanna feel your hair in my hands, going through my fingers.' He gestured doing so across the sofa. 'I wanna kiss your lips, your neck.' Makepeace felt the blood rushing to her cheeks.

Dempsey became even more impassioned. 'I wanna smell the perfume coming up through your clothing.' He paused to regain his breath but their eyes never parted. 'I wanna rip your clothes off and kiss every inch of your body,' he concluded.

'Why don't you?'

There was no trace of play-acting in Makepeace's voice only one of submission. Dempsey drifted towards her. He said nothing only reached out to run his fingers through her hair. She tilted back her head revealing her silken neck and closed her eyes.

She opened them again as a bullet smashed through the window and embedded itself in the wall three foot from Dempsey's head. The moment was gone.

Cathy had gone beserk. As Dempsey's passion had grown so had her anger. No longer was slashing the photographs enough to satisfy her hatred for them. They had to die. She grabbed the rifle from where it was leaning against the wall and flung the window open. Without bothering to take aim she pumped a shot into the living-room window of Dempsey's apartment.

At the sound of the breaking glass Dempsey and Makepeace had both dived behind the sofa. All other emotions were replaced by that of fear, tinged with an element of gratitude that her first shot had been off target. For a few seconds they lay almost on top of each other, trying to gather their thoughts. Makepeace felt Dempsey's breath against her skin and Dempsey breathed in the perfume of her hair.

A second bullet smashed through the window and knocked the baseball bat, that had been awarded to Dempsey for having the highest average in his junior league, off the mantlepiece. They both scrambled to their knees and poked their heads round opposite sides of the sofa. A third bullet ricocheted off one of the blocks of weights on Dempsey's gym equipment and flew back out of the window, whizzing like a firework.

'Look for the flash,' yelled Dempsey. A fourth bullet arrived burying itself in Edgar Allen Poe. Dempsey forced a wry smile. Makepeace saw the flash.

'Fourth floor, corner flat.'

'Let's go then.'

They crawled out of the door and into the hall as a fifth bullet entered the sofa that they had been sheltering behind, emitting a small jet of feathers that floated gently to the floor.

Dempsey and Makepeace sprinted out of the apartment and down the stairs. Half way down the stairs
they bumped into Foley. He moved quickly out of
their way, pressing himself against the wall. He was
surprised to see Dempsey chasing a young woman
down the stairs but he was now used to Dempsey
surprising him and so thought nothing more of it.
Reaching the door of Dempsey's mansion block,
Makepeace peered up at the window from which the
shots had come. It was still open, but there was no
sign of movement inside. They decided to make a run
for the front door of Cathy's apartment block,
diagonally opposite.

They were in luck. Cathy had put down the gun
after the fifth shot. She realized she'd missed and
could see that neither of them were about to pop their
heads up again to give her a bit of extra target
practice. She threw the rifle to the floor and vented
her fury on Dempsey's photographic image again.
She slashed at him wildly, calming occasionally to
delicately gouge out his eyes or in the full length
photographs to castrate him. If she wasn't going to
enjoy him she didn't want anyone else to.

Dempsey and Makepeace threw themselves into
the safety of the mansion block's small porch and
paused for a few seconds to regain their breath. They
pulled their guns from their holsters in unison and
pushed against the door. It was locked. Dempsey
pressed all the entryphone buttons at once. The
speaker crackled into life with various different
versions of 'Hello, who is it?' but before either of
them could reply the electronic door-latch buzzed
open. It was a trick that Dempsey often used when he

was a kid, in order to take a look inside smart condominium blocks; very often there was someone expecting someone so they didn't bother to speak into the answerphone, they just pressed the button to unlock the door. But as they entered into the hall both Dempsey and Makepeace harboured the worrying thought that it might have been Cathy herself who had opened the door for them.

Cathy had indeed heard the ring but she wasn't the one who'd let them in. Rather the ring served to alert her. She stopped slashing at the photographs and began to think almost logically. She knew that they'd be after her now and she concluded that because she'd wanted to kill them that they would also want to kill her. She rushed out of her apartment to the top of the stairwell and looked down. She glimpsed movement at the bottom and threw herself back against the wall. There was no indication that whoever was down there had seen her. She crept slowly up the stairs towards the roof.

Dempsey and Makepeace, weapons at the ready, began to climb the stairs. They leapfrogged from landing to landing covering and overlapping one another. They encountered no one and heard nothing. On reaching the fourth floor they paused. They poked their heads around the corner to check that the corridor was clear. They both jumped as the lights flashed on. Makepeace had leant against the timer button. It did, however, enable them to see more clearly along the corridor. It was empty and all the doors were closed. They made their way along it towards the end door. They stood either side of it and mentally prepared themselves for the entry. They had no idea what lay in wait for them inside. Dempsey remembered his experience with the shotgun in the school two days ago. Makepeace was standing the side of the door that had got blown away on that occasion. He thought of telling her to move but he doubted that Cathy would have had time to set up any kind of booby-trap and if she was standing in the front of the door herself he reckoned that she'd probably choose his side this time, if only for the sake of variety.

He placed his hand on the handle and pushed the door open, every second expecting a deafening explosion and blinding pain. The door swung open and touched gently against the door stop. He rushed in swinging his Magnum from side to side as if to ward off evils spirits. Makepeace followed close on his heels. They stopped in their tracks as they saw in front of them, standing in the middle of the living-room, the walrus. He was even more surprised than they were. He let a bit of hamburger fall from his open mouth. Dempsey and Makepeace were quick to realize their mistake, the internal geography of the block was more complicated than they had assumed.

'Where does the American girl live?' demanded Dempsey.

The walrus swallowed what remained of his hamburger. He pointed blankly to the other side of the corridor. They left.

Dempsey and Makepeace positioned themselves either side of Cathy's door just as they had done previously with the walrus. They entered in the same way. This door wasn't booby-trapped either but they knew at once that it was Catherine Warren's flat. The living-room was empty. Makepeace checked the bedroom and the bathroom to find that she wasn't in there either.

'No sign,' she said, re-entering the living-room.

Dempsey was staring in horror at the photographs on the wall. He pulled one off and examined it more closely, rubbing his fingers across the holes that were his eyes. He dropped the photograph suddenly as if he had been hypnotised into picking up something horribly contagious. Makepeace was also struck dumb by the photographs, by their number and by the obvious venom with which they had been defaced. It was as if inside Cathy's apartment they were also inside her head and could see some of the workings of her mad mind but were provided with no further insight into its machinations.

They soon recovered themselves and the desire to catch her overwhelmed the feeling of horror at discovering her handiwork. They tore their eyes away from the photographs and looked quickly round the rest of the flat. The receiver for the bugging devices lay on the table by the chair from which she obviously watched Dempsey's window. Dempsey looked across at his own apartment. It was hard to remember the events of only a few minutes earlier. The rifle was there also, Makepeace spotted it poking out from beneath the sofa. The only thing that didn't seem to be there was Catherine Warren herself.

'Roof?' suggested Makepeace. Dempsey nodded. He knew that it was always a great mistake to run up on to roofs. It made great cinema but it was lousy for making escapes. But he also knew how easily people were influenced by the movies. Besides, they hadn't passed her on the stairs so she must have gone up onto the roof.

They ran out of the flat and back to the stairwell. The walrus was standing gormlessly in his doorway as they exited. He retreated into the relative safety of his flat as they approached him and peered out timorously again as they passed, more in the manner of a mouse than of the giant mammal that he resembled.

There were two more floors to the mansion block, they climbed them as they had done the previous four, securing them landing by landing. They knew that she didn't have the rifle but they felt that she might well have a hand-gun.

They had just secured the landing between the fifth and sixth floors when, looking out of the window, they caught a glimpse of her running between the chimney stacks of the next door building. They both breathed sighs of relief; she only seemed to have a knife in her hands. The only escape from up there was straight down. Stopping her jumping would now be the problem.

'Try and find a way to get round the back of her,' said Dempsey. Makepeace descended the stairs to do so and Dempsey continued on up towards the roof.

At any other time the view from up there would have been magnificent. Dempsey could have stood admiring it in silence for hours. As it was he burst through the door and rolled across the gravel to the protection of a chimney stack. The sun was setting over London, silhouetting St. Paul's and the building blocks of the city and, in occasional gaps, where the brown waters of the Thames were visible, flashing streaks of bright impressionist orange. Dempsey peeped from behind his chimney stack, at present he was more concerned with his own safety than with the metamorphosis of a dirty grey city.

All seemed clear, so he made his way to the edge of Cathy's mansion block and jumped down onto the roof of the nextdoor building which was one storey lower. There were two other roofs further along that could be reached from the one he was standing on, but neither of them seemed to provide any cover. He concluded that she must be on the roof that he was on at present as there was a long drop to the pavement in the other direction.

He looked about himself. He was surrounded by a veritable labyrinth of sheds, chimney stacks, ventilation units, aerials, and different levels. There were far too many places to hide for his liking. He edged his way to one corner of the roof and began to work his way through it as a grouse beater would. But even before he could reach the corner he found his prey. She appeared from behind a chimney stack between him and the edge clutching her knife to her chest as a child might clutch a doll. She was trembling and her eyes were rimmed with white. Dempsey could see that she was scared, scared and miserable. He put his gun back into his holster and held out his arms towards her to show her that he meant no harm.

'Cathy,' he said as caringly as he could manage. 'Cathy come down with me. Let me take you down.' He reached out his right hand but Cathy didn't seem to understand his words or his gesture. She retreated towards the edge of the building. Dempsey withdrew his hand and stepped back himself, hoping that she would follow his example and move away from the edge, but she stayed where she was. Dempsey didn't worry about her stepping over the edge accidentally as there was a wrought iron fence around the edge of the building but he wanted to get close enough to her so that, if she jumped, he could reach out and grab her.

You kissed me,' she said, half accusingly and half with an air of fond remembrance.

'It was your birthday kiss,' explained Dempsey. He could see that her madness was no longer anything to be feared it was rather something to be pitied. He was no psychoanalyst but he felt he suddenly knew why she had gone mad; it was because she had never been loved, never been able to share her heart with anyone and on her own it had festered. It was her heart not her head that had driven her to madness. He didn't know whether such a thing were possible but he felt that it must be the answer.

'You talked to me,' continued Cathy, as if no one had ever talked to her before. 'You called me love.' Her eyes were full of hurt. 'You bought me roses.'

Dempsey looked at her, his eyes were full of pity. 'I didn't buy you roses,' he said, as if apologizing both for his oversight and her insanity. 'But if you want roses, I'll buy you roses.'

She ignored his offer and his denial. She was remembering all the other wrongs done to her.

'You even had that man play the piano for me.'

Dempsey could see that he wasn't getting through but all he could do was to persist. Perhaps by continually confronting her with the truth it might eventually filter through and she would begin to realize that she was deluding herself.

'There wasn't any piano,' he said quietly, almost sadly.

Again she ignored him.

'Why did you do it?'

Dempsey had no answer to her question, he wished he had but he didn't know what answer she wished to hear.

'Do what? Do what, honey?' He spoke as if speaking to a small child. He was trying to get her to exercise her grievances against him to win some more time and also to help her see that they were pure imagination.

'What things?' he prompted.

Just then Makepeace appeared on the roof behind Cathy. Dempsey tried not to give away her presence. Seeing the confrontation between Dempsey and Cathy, Makepeace also put her gun away. She tried to manoeuvre herself behind Cathy so as she could grab her from behind and prevent her from being able to use the knife.

Meanwhile Cathy was desperately trying to make sense of Dempsey's last question. How could he possibly not know what she was talking about? She looked at him, trying to penetrate his concerned facade. She didn't know how he could possibly be so cruel as to play this game with her. Then, in a flash of sanity, it dawned on her. Perhaps he really didn't know. Her mind was so confused. She no longer knew what was real and what was imagination.

'To her ...' she began trying to explain to Dempsey but was interrupted by the faintest of noises behind her. The tar of the roof was covered with a light scattering of gravel that occasionally crunched under foot. It crunched under foot just as Makepeace arrived within striking distance of Cathy. Cathy twisted sharply and, at the sight of Makepeace creeping up behind her, her madness returned with a vengeance. She lashed out with her knife with a blow that, if it had connected would have decapitated Makepeace.

Dempsey reached out to grab the knife hand but was too slow. Fortunately Makepeace was quicker. She ducked and the knife flashed over her head. The blow not connecting, the momentum of Cathy's body overbalanced her. She fell against the railing which snapped. It did, however, absorb some of her body's momentum. For a second she teetered on the edge of the building, windmilling her arms frantically to try and maintain her balance but her centre of gravity had gone too far.

She began to fall, but the additional second spent on the brink had given Dempsey time to reach her and grab her knife hand just as she fell. The weight of her falling body almost dragged him over too. He collapsed onto his stomach to prevent this happening. His arm felt as if it had been jolted out of its socket. She could only have been eight stone at the most but she felt like twenty, and worse than this she was still clasping the knife, which cut into his wrist with what felt like the force of their combined weights. With every movement she made it cut deeper into his flesh. The pain was unbearable but he knew that he had to bear it. As she looked up at him all her madness seemed to have gone, she was just a desperate woman in fear of losing her life. He had caught hold of the sane woman and the mad woman had fallen to her death. She tried to get a hold with her feet on the side of the building and Dempsey slipped another inch towards the edge of the building himself. Makepeace sat on the back of his legs to weigh him down. It was all that she could do, her arms weren't long enough to help grab hold of Cathy.

'Let go of the knife,' yelled Dempsey. 'I can't hold you.' Cathy tried but Dempsey's grip on her wrist was such that she couldn't release it.

'Help me,' she cried, desperately. She tried to grab onto the side of the building with her free hand but there was nothing to grab hold of. The movement forced the blade of the knife deeper into Dempsey's wrist. He was afraid that it might cut an artery. He put down his own other hand for Cathy to grab.

'Hold onto to me,' he yelled.

Cathy tried to reach the newly proffered hand with her own free hand. But she didn't have the strength. She tried swinging but to no avail. The blood ran down Dempsey's wrist to his hand and then down Cathy's arm. His grip became slippery.

'Hold my hand,' he yelled again, as if the command itself would give her strength. She tried again but only succeeded in loosening his grip on her.

'Let go of the knife.'

The pain was excruciating but he felt that if she dropped the knife then he might be able to grab the fingers of her knife hand with his good hand.

She struggled to release the knife and eventually worked it free. But doing so she was no longer able to keep her hand in a fist. No longer was there anything for Dempsey to get a grip on. Her hand slipped. Dempsey let out a desperate cry. He tried to grip her fingers as they passed through his but the blood made them too slippery. Cathy no longer had the strength to cup her hand into some kind of hook. She fell.

Dempsey watched, helpless, terrified, but unable to turn away. She seemed to fall in slow motion. She didn't cry out, she didn't even struggle. She fell like someone might fall in their dreams and as she fell Dempsey thought he saw a change come over her. He thought he saw her smiling. It was a smile that he'd seen before. It was Theodore Barret's smile. He hoped that it was a good sign of some kind but took the thought no further in case it wasn't. He turned away before she hit the ground but he couldn't help but hear the impact. It was as if a hundredweight of coal had been thrown over the edge, not a human being. He felt sick. Makepeace peered apprehensively over the edge, not through any sense of voyeurism but because people had sometimes been known to survive such falls. Cathy hadn't.

Dempsey and Makepeace sat in silence on the rooftop as the sun set in beautiful ignorance of the mortality of man; the mortality and the fallibility of man. Dempsey and Makepeace had failed. When they were being fired at in Dempsey's living-room, when the adrenalin had been flowing and they were in fear for their own lives, they hadn't really cared whether Cathy lived or died. But having seen that poor lost woman on the rooftop they'd realized that this was someone to save not someone to wreak their vengeance on. They'd failed and Cathy had died.

Makepeace helped Dempsey to his feet and led him down the stairs.

The boys from forensics were late. Apparently a more interesting case had come in at almost exactly the same time. Besides there were no leads to follow up nor fingerprints to take. The case had ended the moment that Catherine Warren had hit the pavement.

The local police had arrived a little earlier and had already asked their questions. They started off by suggesting that Dempsey might have in some way helped Cathy over the edge. Dempsey was too numbed and dazed to argue with them but Makepeace tore a strip off them in his defence and they soon went away with their tails between their legs.

Eventually they were told that they were free to go. Makepeace went with Dempsey back up to his apartment. He was beginning to recover but was obviously still shaken by the experience. As he unlocked the door, the telephone began to ring. He didn't rush for it but walked slowly through the living-room, ignoring the phone in there and picking up the one in the kitchen.

'Yo,' he said half-heartedly.

The phone went dead.

'Not again.' He lifted his head and tried to relax himself by breathing in and out slowly and regularly. The phone started to ring again but this time Makepeace snatched it up before Demsey could get to it.

'Hello,' she said aggressively. Her expression relaxed on hearing a voice on the other end. She held out the phone to Dempsey, covering the mouthpiece. 'It's for you.'

Dempsey looked worriedly at her. 'Who is it?' he asked as if he was amazed that anyone could possibly want to ring him up.

'Thelma.'

His eyes lit up. He took the phone from Makepeace. 'Thelma?' he asked eagerly. Then he remembered that Makepeace was there with him. 'Aunt Thelma — that you?'

Makepeace smiled; he didn't appear to have been too shaken, or, at least, he was easily shaken out of feeling shaken. She picked up her bag and made to go. At the door she turned and waved to Dempsey. He blew her back a kiss.

'When d'you get back into town?' he asked into the telephone, he was beginning to come round to Alexander Graham Bell again.